LOCH NESS HORROR

ERIC S. BROWN

SEVERED PRESS
HOBART TASMANIA

LOCH NESS HORROR

Copyright © 2020 Eric S. Brown

WWW.SEVEREDPRESS.COM

ISBN: 978-1-922551-49-8

LOCH NESS HORROR

Dr. Robert Cline watched the white specks of snow dancing about on the wind which blew in from over the loch. The clouds of the storm didn't completely block out the rays of the moon above. Reflections of its light gleamed on the water that stretched out before him as far as he could see. He pulled his jacket tighter about himself, crossing his arms over his chest. His breath was visible in the cold of the night air. Robert had come to Loch Ness to save the world and couldn't afford to let anything stand in his way.

Sergeant Zayden stood next to Robert, looking out at the water. Zayden had taken command of the platoon of soldiers assigned to watch over him after Captain Reid had met a tragic end shortly after their arrival in Inverness. There was only a handful of those soldiers left now. The journey to Loch Ness had been costly in a great many ways. Robert's long-time assistant, Harrison, had been lost too. It was all he could do to keep his eyes from tearing up at the thought of her. Harrison had been so young and full of life. In a different world, she would have been able to finish up her doctorate and likely replace him as the top of their field one day. Robert chuckled darkly to himself, supposing he was a fool for even thinking about such things.

The surface area of Loch Ness was twenty-two square miles and it contained more water than all the lakes in England and Wales combined thanks to its great depth. The loch was believed to be at least seven hundred and fifty-five feet deep. Robert suspected it was actually far deeper than that. But it wasn't the loch that had brought him here. Like so many others before him, he was searching for its world-famous monster.

Nessie, as most people called her, had first been spotted in April of 1933. Over a century had passed since that initial sighting with tens of thousands more following in its wake. One of the most popular theories was that of Nessie being a Plesiosaur. Others thought she might be a mythical Kelpie. As a member of the Hermetic Order of the Eternal Light, Robert knew that she was neither. The Order's best psionicists had never been able to truly get a read on her but they swore up and down that Nessie was both intelligent and not of this world. Whether she had come to Earth from Outer Space or another dimension was anyone's guess. All attempts to make contact with her by the Order, both in the physical realm and the telepathic, had failed and so their means of dealing with that situation had changed. By the latter half of the 20th century and into the early part of the

21st, the Order had sent numerous squads to capture her. The Order was determined to discover exactly what Nessie was and to know if she was a threat to the human race. There were other ancient entities scattered across the globe, the bulk of which were pure evil or so utterly alien that their mere existence was a threat to mankind's dominance over the Earth. The Hermetic Order of the Eternal Light had been created in 1865 as a classified branch of the United States Secret Service. Their funding came partly from the government, partly from the church, and later from numerous power players in the corporate world. The Order was created to keep the Earth safe from the nightmares that the rest of the world simply couldn't deal with, much less know about.

Basically an organization unto itself, the Order had always been small in its number. At the peak of its power, right before the Fall, the Order was composed of close to three hundred operatives including its administrative and support staff. Robert was the head of its science branch, possessing no PSI talent and having very little field training beyond the basic use of firearms and survival training that was required of all the Order's operatives. If the Order needed real muscle or firepower, it turned to the governments or corporations funding it for those resources just as it sometimes reached out to the church for men of faith to perform exorcisms when psionics alone were not enough go up against an entity that was demonic in nature. The Order had done its job well too. It had stopped a group of vampires from starting a full scale war between humanity and the undead, eked out peace treaties with the various tribes of werecreatures, saved countless souls from the forces of hell, and even entrapped an ancient, world devouring entity at the bottom of the ocean. But no one . . .no one. . .had seen the plague coming. The world was no stranger to global pandemics. The first had happened in 2020 and another in 2027. Both of those had been ordinary viruses, one natural and one man made, and humanity had survived them. Scientists like himself and even the pre-cogs of the Order had been blind to what was about to be unleashed on the Earth. The earliest reported cases were in Africa and the Caribbean. None of them had been taken seriously and by the time they were, it was too late.

All efforts failed to stop the plague from spreading. There was nothing science, psionics, the power of faith, or even military force could do to hold it in check. The necro-plague swept over the world like an ever-growing wildfire. As the governments and corporation ruled sectors of the world fought to hold their ground, the Order joined the fight. Though the Order had always done its best to remain apart from the normal world of man, there was nothing normal about the necro-plague. . . even they were not immune to it.

"The boats shouldn't be too far now if your friends out here managed to get them in place," Sergeant Zayden grunted, taking a drag from the cigarette he held in one hand. In his other, Zayden held tight to the Origin 12 shotgun he carried. There was a Kriss Vector Gen 3, 9mm submachine gun strapped to his back and a Glock holstered on his hip. All of Zayden's men were just as heavily armed. Robert was surprised that any of them had ammo left for their weapons after the hell they had all endured already to reach the loch.

"Any word from the Temple?" Robert asked, instinctively keeping his voice low.

Sergeant Zayden shook his head, dashing Robert's hope that help would be coming. They were okay for the moment and should have what they needed for their search but Robert had no idea how the hell any of them would be getting home. . . assuming there was a home left to go back to.

"Do you think. . .?" Robert started but the corporal cut him off.

"Doesn't matter," Sergeant Zayden snapped. "We have to stay focused, doc."

Robert knew Zayden was right. The lives of everyone left in the world depended on them and the success of their mission here at Loch Ness.

Specialist Payne rushed up to them, his expression grim, addressing Zayden.

"Sir! We got contacts closing in fast from the east," Payne reported.

Robert cocked his head in the direction the corporal had indicated. He could hear the distant snarls and hungry cries of the dead. God only knew how many of the things there were. Their inhuman voices chilled Robert to the bone. He shuddered, looking over at Corporal Zayden.

"We need to get moving, doc!" Sergeant Zayden shoved him. "Go! Go! Go!"

Gunfire erupted behind them as the rear most soldiers opened fire on their pursuers.

Dr. Robert Cline ran for his life, his legs pumping beneath him as he pushed his body to its limits. Sergeant Zayden and the other soldiers could have easily outpaced him but their speed matched his. Their job was to keep him alive. None of them could achieve the mission without him even if they did manage to find and capture the monster in the loch. Robert ran almost blindly, heart pounding inside his chest, sucking in breaths that were ragged gasps. He spotted the dock they were supposed to be headed for and relief washed over him. There were two boats there. Their stark gray and white hulls standing out in sharp contrast to the blackness of the night beneath the half-muted rays of the moon above. They were each nearly eighty-foot-long torpedo boats. Both were heavily armed and additionally outfitted sonar tech that was years ahead of what most people believed possible. There were twin .50 caliber machine guns mounted on the decks of each boat and a surface to surface rocket launcher on its bow. Robert knew they were also equipped with forward torpedo launchers which couldn't be seen beneath the surface of the loch but were certainly there. They were supposed to be carrying depth charges as well. The torpedo boats looked awesome. What didn't look awesome was the fact that Robert couldn't see a single person on their decks or on the dock near them. Where the hell were the troops that had brought them here and got them into position?

Sergeant Zayden grabbed him from behind, bringing Robert to a sudden, lurching halt.

"Hold up!" the sergeant barked.

That was the last fragging thing Robert Cline wanted to do. The snarls and cries of the dead were still ringing out from among the trees of the woods that surrounded this section of the loch and sounded like they were getting closer with each passing second.

Robert looked around to see that three of Sergeant Zayden's

men were missing. There were only four other soldiers with the two of them now. Zayden seemed to read his mind though Robert knew the corporal wasn't any more telepathic than he was himself.

"We can't just go charging onto those boats, doc," Sergeant Zayden cautioned him. "Watson, Hicks, and Shapcot are buying us some time. Let's make fragging sure they aren't dying in vain, doc."

****

Shapcot threw herself against the trunk of a tree, ducking out of sight. Watson was somewhere off to her left and Hicks to her right. She hoped they'd found cover too. There were over a dozen of the dead that were almost on them. Shapcot cursed the dead. The fragging things were supposed to be slow, weren't they? In the black and white zombie film she'd watched with her dad as a kid, the dead seemed barely able to shamble about, these things though. . .they were just as fast as living people, maybe even faster. And they didn't get tired either. Ever. The only advantage the living had over them was that the dead were as stupid as frag. She had lost sight of Hicks entirely but could see Watson from her position. He'd found cover too and was crouching in a patch of brush. As far as Shapcot could tell, both she and Watson had been able to escape being seen by the dead. Now all they had to do was wait for the things to get a little closer. They were running low on ammo and needed to make every one of their shots count.

The dead were tough bastards. They didn't feel pain. Putting a burst of rounds into a dead man's chest might knock him down but it wouldn't keep him there. The only sure way to kill one of the dead was to blow the thing's brains to mush. A lot of folks had learned that fact the hard way during the early days of the necro-plague. God only knew how many had died because they hadn't known.

Sweat slicked Shapcot's body beneath her combat fatigues. She didn't expect to be coming back from this one. This was likely the end. She told herself that at least her life was going to matter. That Dr. Cline guy and the weirdo Order he claimed to be working for were the human race's last hope against the dead. Shapcot had heard the talk. She knew Dr. Cline was supposed to be searching for a cure and if he found it, maybe, just maybe. . .the world could be rebuilt someday back into what it was before the dead rose up, hungry, from their graves.

The dead came bursting out of the depths of the woods into the small clearing that was just beyond her position. It was an almost perfect kill zone. There was no need to signal the others. As soon as they heard her open up on the monsters, they would follow suit. Shapcot took a deep breath, steeling herself, and then stepped out from behind the tree she was using as cover. Scores of eyes that glowed yellow in the darkness fell on her as she raised her weapon. Shapcot had her Vector set to two round bursts, aiming each one that she fired at a deader's forehead. Her first shot cracked open the skull of a thin man with long legs who was wearing the tattered remains of a torn Pink Floyd shirt. His charge was brought to an abrupt halt, nearly flipping over backwards. Without the slightest pause, Shapcot swung the barrel of the Vector around at the next closest of the dead, downing a woman in a bloodstained wedding dress.

Shapcot heard Watson scream. One of the dead had managed to sprint across the small clearing and into melee range with him. The dead woman had flung herself onto him, taking them both to the ground. Watson was twisting about beneath her, struggling to keep her teeth from sinking into the flesh of his face with one hand while the other reached for the knife sheathed on the side of his boot. He had lost his rifle when the dead woman had plowed into him. There was nothing Shapcot could do to help him though. She had her own problems to deal with. . . half a dozen of them. A second wave of the dead had already emerged from the woods, following closely on the heels of the first batch.

The teeth of the dead woman lying atop him clicked together over and over as her mouth opened and closed rapidly. She pressed hard against the flat of his arm that pushed her head upwards away from him. Watson saw nothing human left in the woman's eyes, only a burning hunger. His knife slid free of its sheath. He brought it up, trying to sink into the side of the dead woman's head. Missing his target as the two of them struggled, the knife entered her neck instead. Putrid, black blood splattered out of her rotting body onto his hand and the sleeve of his combat fatigues. Watson twisted the blade inside the woman, trying to work it loose and yank it out. The woman didn't react at all to the wound he had dealt her. She was beyond experiencing pain. Unfortunately, Watson wasn't. A stick that lay in the dirt under him stabbed into his back as they fought. Taken by surprise by the sudden surge of pain piercing into him, his arm that was keeping the dead woman off of him slipped downward. The woman leaned in, her teeth raking away a chunk of flesh from his left cheek. Seizing the moment, the dead woman grabbed hold of Watson's arms, forcing them back, so that she could get at his throat. Her teeth chomped into the soft flesh there, severing his carotid artery. Watson's bright, red blood exploded all over her.

Shapcot retreated as she continued to pour fire into the approaching dead, downing one of the creatures with every two round burst her Vector spat. She hated giving up any ground but there was nothing for it. It was either that or be overrun. There were just too many of the dead coming out of the trees. The bodies of the dead they'd already killed did nothing to give pause to the creatures behind them. The dead were incapable of feeling fear.

Hicks stumbled out of the brush beside her. He was bleeding badly from a bite on his right arm but was far from out of the fight. There was nothing left to lose for him. The bite had sealed his fate. Even if they somehow escaped and made it back to the others, Hicks was dead. There would be nothing for him but a merciful bullet to the head. The two of them concentrated their fire at the dead as the creatures came bounding towards them. A stream of rounds ripped up the stomach of a dead woman before working their way up to reduce her head to a mess of exploding pulp. Hicks was having difficulty steadying his weapon with one arm barely functional. He flung his Vector away and drew the Glock holstered on his hip. The pistol might not have the firepower of the Vector but at least Hicks could aim his shots with it.

Shapcot lunged to the right as a dead man who had closed the distance between them made a grab at her. He was too close to get a good shot at him with her Vector. She slammed its butt in his mouth with a rewarding crunching sound. Fragments of broken teeth and black blood flew from the dead man's mouth as his head was knocked to the right. Before he could recover, Shapcot swept his legs from under him, sending the dead man toppling to the ground. Her Vector barked as Shapcot put a two round burst into the center of his forehead. The bastard wouldn't be getting back up.

Hicks dropped another deader with a shot that entered its head through the creature's left eye socket and exited its skull in a spray of bits of shattered bone, black blood, and brain matter. Swinging his Glock around, Hicks got off another shot that slammed into the shoulder of another dead man that was coming towards him in a full out sprint. The shot wasn't enough to stop the snarling corpse. The dead man rammed into Hicks like an NFL linebacker, locking its arms about his waist. Hicks grunted as his breath left his lungs. His back smashed into the trunk of a tree and sent his Glock flying as he lost his grip on it. The dead man reared up in front of Hicks, sinking the tips of its fingers into his abdomen. Hicks screamed as the creature pulled its hands apart, opening up his stomach. Purple, red slicked strands of his intestines poured out of Hicks as he struggled to force the dead man away from him. Hicks drew his left hand back and punched the dead man in the side of the head with all the strength he could muster. The blow staggered the creature but the fight was already lost. Hicks wasn't able to press his attack. The pain he was in was simply too much. His vision blurred and his head swam, the world spinning around him. Shapcot gave him mercy. Hicks likely felt the two rounds from her Vector that cracked open his forehead in an explosion of gore.

A pair of dead men closed in on Shapcot, one coming in at her from each side. Her Vector clicked empty as she squeezed its trigger. There was no time to reload the weapon. She let the gun fall from her hands, whirling about to make a run for it. Shapcot cursed as her legs pumped beneath her. She could hear the snarls of the dead men behind her. Somewhere, far in the distance, Shapcot heard the powerful engine of a boat roar to life. The sound brought her comfort. It meant that she, Hicks, and Watson had succeeded in buying the others the time they had needed. There was no point in heading in the direction of the boat though. It would be long gone before she ever reached the dock. Shapcot changed the path of her flight, zagging to the right. One of the two dead men on her heels tripped over something as the thing tried to follow her and fell, sprawling out onto the ground. The other was drawing closer with each passing second though. The realization that she wasn't going to be able to outrun the creature was a harsh one but just maybe she could outsmart it.

Shapcot darted around the trunk of a tree in a sharp turn without slowing her pace. The dead man wasn't able to make the turn and lumbered on past her. Shapcot jerked up her pistol and fired a round into the backside of the man's skull, sending him to hell with a single shot. The sound of her Glock firing gave away her position to the rest of the dead in the area. Shapcot saw a large group of the dead making their way back from the direction of the dock towards her. Their yellow eyes glowed bright with hunger and an inhuman rage in the dimness of the moonlight. She yanked a grenade from a pouch on her combat vest, pulling the pin, and lobbed it at the approaching creatures. The blast seemed to shake the woods around her as it lit up the night in a bright flash of fiery white. She didn't see what effect it had on the monsters, Shapcot was already moving again. Her breath came in ragged gasps as Shapcot pushed herself on.

A dead woman came out of seemingly nowhere. The woman's jagged fingernails drew blood as the raked across Shapcot's cheek. Shapcot spun about to engage the dead woman. Lashing out with a kick that planted one of her combat boots in the center of the dead woman's chest, Shapcot heard a pop and a cracking noise as the woman's sternum gave way. Hurled backwards from the force of the kick, the dead woman landed on her back. As the dead woman began to shove herself back onto her feet, Shapcot fired her Glock directly into her face. The dead woman slumped back onto the ground, brain matter leaking out of her head into the grass. Shapcot lurched into a run, again knowing that she couldn't keep this up much longer.

Sprinting away from the loch now, Shapcot ejected the nearly spent magazine of her Glock and slammed a fresh one home. She mumbled a prayer for Sergeant Zayden and the others. In every direction she looked around her, Shapcot could see burning, yellow eyes. The dead were all around her now. There was nowhere left to run to and she lacked the strength to keep fighting her way through the creatures. Shapcot skidded to a halt in the center of a small clearing, deciding to make her stand there. Her Glock cracked again and again in rapid succession as she sent one deader to hell after another until the weapon clicked empty. Several of the dead reached her at the same time. Cold hands grabbed hold of her, jerking Shapcot in different directions. Jagged fingernails tore open the skin of her arms as she fought to break free of the hands that clutched her. One of the dead dropped to the ground, taking a large bite out of her right thigh. Shapcot screamed as blood spurted over the creature's swollen lips and rotting face. Its hold on her caused Shapcot to lose her balance. She went down, dead men and women still clinging to her. Shapcot's legs kicked in desperation at the dead as she caught hold of the lower jaw of a dead man that was trying to sink his teeth into her. She wrenched the dead man's jaws apart, snapping them apart at their joints. Her combat helmet had come loose and had been flung from her head in the struggle. Another dead man grabbed Shapcot, decaying fingers catching a handful of her hair, and smacked her head hard against the ground. That was the end of her struggle. Shapcot went limp, on the verge of passing out, as the dead man claimed his prize. His teeth ripped at the softer flesh of her lips and eyelids, tearing them away. Other dead men and women bit at her arms and legs. The last sounds Shapcot heard before she died was the sickening smacking of lips as the dead chewed upon the still warm feast of her body.

****

Sergeant Zayden and his four remaining soldiers couldn't secure both of the torpedo boats in the amount of time afforded to them. As thus, they went aboard the *TK* and left *The Thunder* where she bounced on the waves next to the dock. Despite the length of the torpedo boats, their interiors were small with limited space. There was a CIC/Control room, a circular room that served as a galley, mess, and sleeping quarters for up to eight people, and an engine room at the rear.

The thin, slick layer of accumulated snow on the *TK's* deck had patches of red in it that could only be human blood. There was black goo smeared on the boat's walls too. It was easy to see there had been a battle here not long ago which begged the question, where the hell was everyone? The boats' crew should have been present even if the squad of soldiers assigned to protect them weren't. Robert Cline knew that the elders of the Order of the Eternal Light would have surely sent such troops with the boats' crews. That just made sense with so much at stake. All the cities and towns surrounding the loch had been overrun by the dead much like everywhere else in the world. Yet, there wasn't a single body aboard the *TK* or on the dock near her either. Whatever had taken out her crew and the crew of *Thunder* as well must have moved the bodies for some reason. It was implausible to think that all of them had been infected and risen to go howling off into the night in search of prey. Even if that were the case, as dumb as the risen dead were, there would surely have been some of the creatures trapped inside the *TK* unable to navigate their way out of her interior and onto her deck.

On the upside, the *TK* was very much intact and already

powered up, her engine humming quietly. She was ready and waiting for them just like they had been promised the boat would be. With the boat secured, Heddon and Payne rushed to take up positions at the pair of twin-mounted .50 calibers on her deck. Malor hung back, staying aft, the barrel of her Kriss Vector aimed at the trees lining the shore beyond the dock. Sergeant Zayden dragged Robert along with him into the *TK*'s interior with Jace following after them. All of them had received rushed, basic instruction on the operation of PT boats like the *TK* and *The Thunder*.

"Jace! Get us moving!" Sergeant Zayden barked.

The hum of the *TK's* engine cranked up into a full out roar as the boat surged forward, leaving the dock behind. All of them knew that once they were truly out upon the water of the loch, the dead would no longer be a threat. The dead were only able to float for a brief amount of time until their lungs filled up with water and then they sunk like stones. Sure, the dead didn't breathe but they did snarl, moan, and sometimes chomped at empty air. Water would get into their lungs fast and pull the things down. In shallow water, that might be a problem but the depth of Loch Ness was staggering. When they went down, the dead wouldn't be coming back up unless they were close enough to a section of the shore line that they could manage to walk or climb up.

Robert grabbed the edge of one of the CIC's stations to keep from losing his balance from the boat's sudden start. He looked over at Sergeant Zayden. The sergeant was scowling despite their success in getting to the boat and escaping the army of the dead. Robert knew their situation was still very grim. With no word from the Temple, they were on their own out here. The lack of contact with the Temple begged the question as to why they couldn't reach it. Their comm. gear was fully functional and there was no interference to speak of. The Temple should be answering them. Everyone back there was fully aware of just how critical to the survival of the human race their mission here was. Had something happened? Could the Temple have been overrun by the dead? Robert couldn't bring himself to accept that conclusion. The Temple was one of the most heavily fortified bases in existence and not just through conventional means either. There were both psionic barriers and magical wards in place guarding it.

Jace slowed the boat now that it was out fully on the loch and well beyond the reach of the dead.

"Okay, Dr. Cline," Sergeant Zayden said, "it's your show now. How do we find this monster of yours?"

Robert shrugged. "There was supposed to be PSI agent

waiting on us at the dock with the boats. That would have been the easiest means of proceeding."

Sergeant Zayden grunted. "Well, there wasn't, was there?"

Sighing, Robert shook his head. "No. That means we're going to have to rely on the upgraded sonar that was installed on this boat."

"I suggest you get to it then, doc," Sergeant Zayden ordered him.

Robert moved to the console on the far side of the CIC that had been set up for using the boat's sonar arrays. Powering it up, Robert ran a quick sweep of the loch around the *TK*. His eyes bugged as Robert stared at the screen in utter shock.

"What is it, doc?" Sergeant Zayden asked, deep concern in his voice.

"I've got a contact," Robert answered.

"What? Already?" Sergeant Zayden stared at him.

"A big one too," Robert nodded. "It's CBDR. . . coming straight at us."

"Evasive action!" Sergeant Zayden barked.

"Frag," Jace muttered, revving up the *TK's* engine to full power. The boat surged forward, angling away from the inbound contact.

"It's matching our speed and veering towards us," Robert

said.

"Can we outrun that thing?" Sergeant Zayden asked.

Robert shook his head. "I find that highly unlikely."

"Sir!" Heddon's voice rang out over the ship's comm. She was manning one of the forward mounted, twin .50 calibers on the *TK*'s deck and calling to them through the radio of her combat helmet. "I've got a visual on something fragging huge and it's coming at us fast."

"Just how big is this thing?" Sergeant Zayden frowned.

"From the readings I am getting, the contact is over eighty feet long and has to weigh several tons based on the amount of water it's displacing," Robert told him.

"That's way larger than any Plesiosaur should be, doc," Jace commented.

"No one ever said this thing was a Plesiosaur," Robert shrugged. "That's just a widely popular theory without any hard evidence to back it up."

"Whatever this thing is, it's coming straight at us, doc," Sergeant Zayden pressed him.

"Without a PSI, we have no means of trying to make contact with it," Robert admitted.

"I can't just let that thing ram through this boat, Dr. Cline," Sergeant Zayden snapped. "Heddon, Payne! Open fire on that fragging thing and let it know that it's picked the wrong ship to mess with!"

Robert breathed a sigh of relief at the course of action Sergeant Zayden had taken. The sergeant could have just as easily engaged the approaching creature with the *TK*'s rockets or torpedoes. Either of those stood a much greater chance of killing it. Robert didn't believe the .50 calibers would. They might hurt it, yes, but odds were, they wouldn't do more than wound the creature.

The creature was coming in from Heddon's side of the boat. Strands of her long, brown hair had slipped loose from beneath her helmet and fluttered about in the wind that blew over the loch. Snow was still falling but the loch itself wasn't frozen. Heddon's green eyes locked onto the approaching giant form just below the water's surface. She couldn't make out much more about it than its general shape. The thing was long, really long, and slim. It was shaped much like a snake. Her hands clutched the firing controls of her .50 caliber tightly as she opened up in the thing's direction. The twin .50 calibers roared bright orange, tracer rounds streaking through the darkness. Heddon did her best to keep her fire just ahead of the creature's position rather than aiming for its body. Her goal was to discourage the thing from ramming into the *TK*, not kill it, though she heavily doubted the twin .50 caliber could.

The creature dove deeper into the water, increasing its already unbelievable speed. Water exploded upwards towards the night sky as the monster resurfaced on the other side of the boat. It had gone under it. Payne cried out in sheer terror as he brought the barrels of his own twin .50 calibers around to engage the creature.

"Hold your fire!" Heddon yelled at him but if Payne heard her, the man gave no sign of it. His .50 calibers continued in a booming chatter, spraying a continuous stream of twelve hundred rounds a minute at the creature. The surface of the water churned where the bullets entered it, Payne's fire following the retreating, giant creature.

"Frag it!" Sergeant Zayden cursed inside the CIC. "Payne! Hold your fire, man! That's an order!"

"The creature is going deep again," Robert said, keeping his eyes on the sonar screen.

"You think he hit it?" Jace asked no one in particular.

"I'd say so," Robert nodded. "It's swinging around to come at us again."

"Great," Sergeant Zayden raged. "If that thing wasn't ticked off at us before you can dang well bet it is now."

Payne had finally stopped shooting.

"What the hell was up with that?" Heddon shouted over at him.

"Didn't you see that thing?" Payne yelled back at her.

Apparently, Payne had gotten a much better look at the creature than she had from the expression on his face. He looked scared out of his mind. Payne wasn't an easy guy to rattle but whatever he had seen seemed to have him on the edge of crapping his pants. His cheeks were pale and his eyes wide. Both of them heard the sound of the loch's surface stirring. Several hundred yards from the *TK*, the water parted as a giant head rose up out of it. The thing's head was the size of a small car. Heddon saw that she was wrong about the thing's body. It wasn't smooth and sleek as a snake's now. Numerous tentacles were unfolding from it and whipping about wildly in the air. Two eyes that blazed like purple suns stared back at her as she looked over the creature. . . the monster. The thing's face was flat and horrid. Just looking into it made Heddon sick to her stomach. It took a lot of willpower to fight down the vomit rising in her throat. She'd never seen anything as repulsive in her life. The creature opened its mouth revealing rows upon rows of gleaming, razor edged, pointed teeth. The creature let loose a shrill cry that rose in pitch and volume as it droned on. The cry was so intense that both Payne and Heddon dropped to their knees behind their mounted .50 calibers, slapping their hands over their ears. Inside the *TK,* the others did the same. Sergeant Zayden fought against the pain of the noise, attempting to order Jace to lock onto the creature with the boat's rockets and blow it back to whatever hell the thing had rose up from but couldn't. The creature's shrill cry continued. The thick, reinforced glass of the boat's windows fractured and cracked before blowing apart. Shards of glass flew inward into the CIC. One of them sliced open a long gash across Jace's arm. Another struck Sergeant Zayden, dead on, in the center of his throat. Sergeant Zayden stumbled backwards, rivers of bright red blood pouring down the front of his combat fatigues. His right hand raised up, fingers clawing at the shard of glass in his throat, but he was unable to yank it out. Sergeant Zayden's corpse thudded onto the floor of the CIC next to where Robert was crouching with his hands clasped over his ears. Robert barely noticed. His entire world was nothing more than the crippling pain of the noise. . . but it was more than just the noise. Something more was piercing his brain, shoving its way into his mind. Robert opened his mouth to scream as the entire world around him seemed to light up in a blinding flash of white.

****

The screaming and gunfire outside had died away to the sound of a single, whimpering voice. Cato sat with his back pressed to the metal of the door that led into the corridor. It was just barely cracked open on one side where it had slammed shut on Shasa when the Temple went into emergency lockdown. The impact was enough to kill her instantly but not enough to completely sever her body in two. Her legs still twitched every few seconds or at least they looked like they did. Sitting in the puddle of blood that spilled out from her corpse, Cato wasn't entirely sure what was real anymore and what wasn't. All he did know for sure was that he couldn't just keep sitting where he was. He had to get up and get moving before the dead discovered him.

Cato was still in shock and he knew it. The dead never should have been able to breach the Temple. The Temple was a state of the art, subterranean base built to withstand a direct hit from a nuke. The blast doors of its exterior, above ground entrance were four feet thick and reinforced by both magical wards and a continually active energy field of the Order's own design. Half a dozen clairvoyants and pre-cogs were constantly on watch for dangers to the Temple along with sensor tech that was well beyond that in use by the world's leading militaries. Nothing unwanted should ever have been able to breach the Temple. The best Cato could figure was that something terrible had gone wrong with the attempt to open a portal to the shores of Loch Ness. Psychoportation was a dangerous means of transit, used only in the direst and most desperate circumstances. The end of the human race certainly classified as such and that was why such an attempt had been made. In one of the Temple's two massive hangar bays, the Order's only psychoportist, Ryker, and many of its other most powerful PSIs and mages had gathered, combining their power, to open such a portal. They had succeeded in opening *something* and wherever their portal led to, it was still open now. Cato could feel its energy like a dull throbbing inside his mind. The dead that was inside the Temple could only have come from it.

In the end, Cato supposed it didn't matter how the dead had gotten in or where they were coming from. The things had caught everyone off-guard, tearing through the Temple in a bloody rampage before any kind of organized force could be assembled to stop the creatures. He had been in his quarters when the alarm klaxons began to blare throughout the Temple and was still stuck there now. Everything just happened so fast.

Only being recruited by the Order a few months ago, Cato was technically still an initiate though he was doing the work of a senior agent. Like the rest of the world, the Order was hit hard by the virus. The Order had sought him out because supposedly he was one of the more powerful PSIs of the current generation. Cato thought that was a bunch of crap and had sucked in the training he had been given so far. His instructors never told him exactly what they thought he was capable of but the first classes for all recruits were basic telepathic protection barriers and sending/receiving. Those were required for every PSI in the Order whether they were telepaths or not. No one wanted secrets being stolen or agents being turned because they couldn't keep an enemy PSI out of their head.

Cato had tried reaching out to Pete, his current instructor, but that experience had dang well stopped him from trying to reach anyone else. Pete was gone. . .dead, one of the hungry, primal monsters tearing through the base in search of prey. Making contact with Pete's mind had been one of the worst things Cato had ever experienced. It was like being chained up and thrown into an icy lake while at the same time being doused in gasoline and set on fire. There were no thoughts in Pete's head, nothing left of his mind or his soul. There was only burning hunger and the cold, emptiness of death. Cato had nearly been sucked so deep into it that he'd almost become trapped in Pete's head. There were stories in the Order about PSIs who tried to read the dead or the dying, before the time of the risen dead, who had been lost that way. Cato shuddered where he crouched with his back against the door and was thankful to God that he had been able to break free of Pete's mind.

In his right hand, Cato clutched his Maxim 11 pistol so tightly that his knuckles were white. The weapon was one that only agents of the Order carried. It was a prototype machine pistol with a secondary, mini shotgun barrel below its primary barrel. The shotgun barrel was only capable of a single, 12 gauge shot but that was often more than enough to stop an enemy from coming at you. The Maxim 11 machine pistol had three fire modes- single shot, three round burst, and full auto. The Maxim 11's magazine contained thirty-three, compressed 9mm bullets. That was a bloody, fragging lot for a pistol. Sometimes, the level of tech the Order had available to it just blew Cato's mind. And there wasn't much that the Order didn't have, heck, they even had power armor and mechs though both of those were rarities and seldom used because of their costs. Cato wished he had a full out mech suit right now. The dead would be powerless to hurt him and even stop him from just walking out of the Temple if he did. With his current level of clearance, Cato didn't know where the mechs and power armor were stored inside the Temple, much less how to operate them. They were normally used by agents who weren't PSIs and as thus his training hadn't extended to anything in regards to them other than mentions that such tech existed for the Order's most dangerous missions.

As the world fell, several units of the United States military had withdrawn into the Temple, taking shelter with the Order's still surviving operatives and staff. Cato wondered how many of them were still alive now. Not many, he guessed, not with the dead inside the Temple.

Shaking his head to clear his thoughts, Cato took a deep breath and stood up. He turned around to face the door that led out into the corridor. The whimpering outside had stopped now too. Whoever had been doing it had to have died because Cato heard a low growl from the other side of the cracked open door. His knife was buried in the side of Sasha's skull. Cato had used it to give her mercy before she reanimated after being killed by the emergency lockdown of the Temple's doorways. Reaching down, he wrenched it free, wiping its blade on the leg of his pants, and shoved the knife back into its sheath, figuring that he was going to need every weapon he had as he headed out of his quarters. Thankfully, the Temple's main power was still on so that he wouldn't have to try and shove the door leading into the corridor the rest of the way open. Instead, he moved to the control panel on the wall near it and typed in his passcode, overriding the lockdown protocol. That trick wasn't going to work for any of the Temple's exits but would allow him to move around its interior.

As the door of his quarters slid open, Cato saw Agent Blythe standing in the corridor outside. She was clearly dead. Most of her right cheek was gnawed away and the front of her jacket and shirt were drenched with blood. Blythe's head whipped around in his direction from the sound of the door swishing open. Her eyes glowed an eerie shade of yellow that made Cato think of the fires of hell itself. Blythe's lips parted in a feral snarl that showed her teeth as Cato took aim at her with his Maxim 11, shifting it into a two-handed grip as he fired. The pistol bucked in his hands, spitting a three round burst at Blythe. The bullets ripped into her chest sending blood and bits of her flesh flying. They punched a hole through her sternum, splattering slimy, black gore onto the corridor wall behind where she stood. Blythe was knocked off balance by the burst but not knocked down. She staggered sideways, trying to right herself. Cato cursed himself for not remembering to aim for her head. His heart was thundering against his ribcage and sweat, born of fear, slicked his skin. Blythe was the first deader Cato had ever seen up close and personal. He had dealt with Sasha before she turned.

Blythe regained her footing and sprang at him, screeching like some kind of wild animal. Cato fired again. This time, Blythe's head seemed to explode as three rounds punched into and through her forehead. Her corpse hit the floor and lay there twitching, a puddle of infected, black blood forming around her shattered skull. Cato quickly looked up and down the corridor to make sure Blythe had been the only one of the dead close by. Whether she was or not, he knew more would be coming, his shots had echoed loudly in the tight space of the corridor. Cato felt sick as he realized that those shots had just told all the dead within earshot exactly where he was. The Temple's command center was two levels up and it was where he needed to go. If there were any other members of the Order left alive, that's where they would most likely be holed up.

Cato took off running along the corridor towards where he knew the closest elevator was located. Since Cato had very stupidly blown any chance of sneaking through this level of the Temple unnoticed with how he had dealt with Blythe, speed was his only option now. Rounding a corner, Cato skidded to an abrupt halt. There were two dead men ahead of him, between him and the elevator. They looked to have been just milling about until he had shown up but they sprang into action at the sight of him. Both of them came charging towards Cato as he backpedaled, trying to put some distance between himself and the two dead men. Before he could bring his Maxim 11 up and get off a shot, a long burst of fully automatic fire rang out. The dead men's bodies jerked about as high caliber rounds punched through them and flung them into the corridor's wall. As soon as it stopped, Cato didn't hesitate. He walked over to the dead men, putting a single round into each of their heads.

"Well, frag me," a woman dressed in standard issue, Order combat armor laughed. "Is that you, Cato? How the hell are you still alive?"

It took a moment for Cato to recognize the woman. Her name was Romona Rory, a senior agent of the Order, who had given him his tour of the Temple when he had first been recruited. Cato hadn't seen her since. She was way out of his league in terms of rank, experience, and power.

"Yes, ma'am," Cato stammered. "It's me."

Romona grunted and shook her head.

"Of all the people in this Temple. . ." she muttered.

"Ma'am, we've got to get out of here," Cato said.

"Really, kid?" Ramona chuckled darkly. "Ya think?"

Another deader, this one a woman in an army uniform, rounded the corner behind Cato and rushed towards him, arms outstretched, lips parted in a snarl. Romona popped it with a head shot that sent the dead woman toppling over backwards. Her reflexes left Cato in awe.

"Come on," Romona shouted, racing over to the elevator's

controls. Cato was afraid it had been locked down like the Temple's exterior doors and might not respond to his passcodes. Romona's were of a much higher clearance level than his own. The elevator's doors opened. He hurried inside it after her, the doors sliding closed behind him.

"I was trying to reach the command center," Cato said as he ejected the magazine of his Maxim 11 and slammed a fresh one into the weapon, not wanting to chance running out of ammo if they ran into a larger group of the dead.

"That place is a bloodbath, kid," Romona told him. "No point in going there unless you want to be torn apart by those things out there."

Cato swallowed hard, knowing that if the command center had fallen, then the entire base really was lost. He didn't know what to say so Cato just stared at Romona like a sad puppy waiting for its master to lead it.

"Buck up, kiddo," Romona ordered him. "We've lost another battle, sure, but the war is far from over."

"Will you please stop calling me that," Cato spoke up, suddenly finding courage he didn't know he had.

"Calling you what?" Romona laughed.

"I'm not a kid. You're barely older than I am, ma'am," Cato said.

"And if I were a psycho-metabolist, how the frag could you know that?" Romona challenged him.

"But you're not," Cato shot back at her. "I know who you are, ma'am. You're one of the Order's strongest telekinetics. Frag, you're a bloody legend."

Romona grinned. "You're right about the TK part anyway. That legend crap. . ."

"Ma'am, if we're not heading for the command center, where are we headed?" Cato asked, noticing that the elevator was descending instead of going up.

"We're going to the hangar where those idiots opened a portal," Romoma answered.

"Why in the hell are we going there?" Cato snapped, forgetting himself and just how much Romona outranked him. "There's got to be an army of the dead in that hangar."

Romona shook her head. "Doubt it. Those things are spread out all over now. What point would there be in those things hanging around a hangar?"

"How can you know there's not more of them still coming through the portal?" Cato asked.

"Look, Cato, that portal is our only real hope of getting out of this place and getting to somewhere that we can hopefully make a difference," Romona explained. "They were supposed to be opening one to Scotland where Dr. Cline's team is going after the Loch Ness Monster."

"I heard about that. Dr. Cline believes the monster is carrying antibodies that can act as a vaccine against the dead virus, maybe even cure it outright," Cato said. "I mean how could he even know something like that?"

"The Order has made contact with the Loch Ness Monster before," Romona told him.

"Not much. I've read the files." Cato glared at her, trying not to show the frustration he was feeling.

"You've read the files?" Romona snorted. "You're a newbie, Cato. Do you really think they gave you access to everything? The Order had made contact with the monster before. Trust me, you don't want to tick that thing off but this time we might not have a choice if Dr. Cline can't convince it to save the human race."

"Huh," Cato grunted.

"Now come on, we ain't gonna get to that portal by standing here chit-chatting," Romona said and got moving. The elevator had reached its destination a while back but she had kept the doors closed so they could have their talk. They slid open as she stabbed a thumb on the button that controlled them. Just as Cato had feared, there was a pack of dead people waiting for them outside. He shouldn't have worried though because Romona was with him. The powerful TK swept a hand through the air, unleashing a wave of physically manifested mental energy that smashed into the group of the dead with the force of a runaway eight-wheeler. The bones of the dead snapped inside their bodies even as they were picked up and tossed away from the elevator's doors. One of the dead flew far enough to slam into the far wall of the corridor. Its body splattered apart as the creature struck the wall in an explosion of gore.

"Holy. . ." Cato mumbled, looking over at Romona in awe once more.

"Come on, kid! There will be more of those things coming!" Romona shouted, dashing out of the elevator. Cato followed after her.

****

Dr. Robert Cline came awake, sucking in air. There was water with it. He started sputtering and coughing, fighting not to drown. His arms splashed about madly against the surface of the loch. Somehow, he had managed to get on a life jacket, either that or someone had put one on him. Either way, it was all that was keeping him alive. His eyes were blinking rapidly, trying to adjust from coming awake so suddenly. The water was so cold, his body felt like it was encased in ice. He looked up and saw the *TK*. The torpedo boat was fifty feet or more away from his position. It was fire. The entire mass of the boat that was above the waterline was ablaze, yellow and orange flames dancing and flashing in the darkness of the night. Snow was still falling but hadn't appeared to have picked up any.

Robert looked around, gulping down another mouthful of the loch's water, searching for anyone else who might have survived nearby. There was no one. He was alone in the water and freezing to death very quickly. Something registered in his ears beyond the sound of his own desperate splashing and the crackling and popping of the TK's flames. It was the sound of an approaching engine. Another ship came into view, swinging wide around the burning remains of the *TK*. The sharp white of the boat's hull gleamed in the light of the fire and the dim moon above. Robert could see people on its forward deck frantically moving about. The boat looked to be some kind of small, civilian yacht. Someone aboard it threw a life preserver into the water near him. Robert fought through his panic and got himself together enough to swim for the floating orange ring. His hands grabbed onto it.

"Just hold on, mate!" a voice yelled at him. "We're going to get you out of there!"

The people on the boat were pulling in the life preserver and him with it. Robert kept his grip on the orange ring as he felt hands lifting his body up and out of the frigid water. They dropped him on the deck of the yacht. He lay there, shivering, and fighting to breathe.

"Hit it!" another voice shouted. "Get us the hell out of here, Saul!"

Robert heard the yacht's engine roaring as it surged onward across the loch before the world went dark before his eyes and he passed out again.

This time, when Robert woke up, he was warm. There was no water trying to pull him down or splashing into his mouth. Instead, he lay in a small bed, covers over him, keeping his body warm. The room around him was quaint. He could tell from the bend in the ceiling and feeling of movement beneath him that he was still aboard the yacht that had picked him up. The room's only door opened as a handsome, young man dressed in jeans and a Billy Idol shirt with spiked hair entered.

"Hey, mate," the young man grinned. "Good to see that you're awake."

"Where am I?" Robert croaked, his voice little more than a weak whisper. Still, the young man heard him.

"You're aboard the *Lady Freedom*," the young man answered. "My name is Weston. I didn't catch yours."

"Doctor. . ." Robert started and then coughed.

"You're a doctor?" Weston gawked at him.

"Dr. Robert Cline," he finished.

"Dang," Weston's grin grew. "We really lucked out."

"What . . . what the hell happened?" Robert asked.

Weston gave a humorous snort, "Man, we were hoping you could tell us that. Something fragged up that boat you had been on. . . bad. It blew as we were pulling away from it. Our skipper took some shrapnel in the arm. You think you might be able to help him?"

"I'm not that kind of doctor," Robert told him.

"But you can try?" Weston asked.

"Sure," Robert nodded. His strength was returning to him. Weston moved to reach in a cabinet near the bed that he was lying in and produced a bottle of water from it, offering it to him. Robert took it and drank nearly half of it in a single gulp.

"Whoa mate," Weston cautioned him. "Take it easy. You look like you've been through hell. You don't want to push it."

"I'm fine," Robert said, handing the bottle of water back to Weston and then trying to push himself up from the bed. He got halfway up before the world started spinning.

"You don't look fine," Weston said, seemingly amused by his plight.

Robert stopped moving long enough to find his center and let the dizziness pass and then swung his feet off the bed onto the floor. Looking down, Robert realized someone had changed his clothes. His combat fatigues and boots were gone, replaced by jeans, a loose shirt, and sneakers.

Weston must have picked up on what was going through his head because he said, "Yeah, mate, sorry about that. That stuff you were wearing was soaked. If we had left you in them, you'd be dead now."

"Thanks," Robert grumbled. He was grateful for his life being saved but all of a sudden felt very naked without the Glock he'd been carrying. Civilization was already pretty much a thing of the past and even if the people of the *Lady Freedom* had saved him, that didn't mean he could trust them. There was too much at stake. The fate of the human race itself was resting on his shoulders.

"You want to tell me what happened now?" Weston pressed him. "Were you guys boarded by dead people when you left the dock or maybe did one of your people turn or something?"

"What?" Robert snapped more harshly than he should have. "There weren't any of the dead on the *TK.*-1483973646 "

"The *TK?*" Weston frowned. "That's a fragging weird name for a boat, even a military one."

"I'm not military," Robert shook his head, standing up.

"Could have fooled me, mate," Weston said, his hand slipping beneath his shirt. It came back out holding a 9mm which was aimed at Robert. "Why don't you just sit back down on that bed and let us finish the talk we're having, mate? I'd hate to have anything untoward happen to you, if you take my meaning."

"None of us have time for this, Weston," Robert remained standing. "There's a lot more going on than you know about."

"Frag yeah there is." Weston raised the barrel of his 9mm more level with Robert's chest. "So why don't you start talking, doc. You and I are going to get some things cleared up and then you're going to help my skipper, unless you'd like to go back into the water that is."

Robert was weighing up in his mind whether to make a grab for Weston's gun or just slump back onto the edge of the bed and tell him everything when the door to the small room opened again.

"Weston!" a big, burly man, with shoulders so wide Robert questioned if he could even fit through the tight doorway into the room with them, barked. "Put that gun away!"

Looking panicked, Weston flipped on the pistol's safety and

shoved it back beneath his belt.

"Sorry, skipper. I was. . ." Weston whimpered.

"Stow it, kid," the big man growled. "Both of you get your butts up out of there and up here pronto."

Robert hesitated.

"Now!" the big man ordered him.

Weston moved aside to let Robert head up first. The two of them emerged from the small room onto the deck of the yacht. Snow was whipping about them on the wind. The big man shrugged off the coat he was wearing and handed it to Robert. He quickly put it on. The coat's right sleeve was slashed open near its shoulder and felt warmer than the rest of it. Robert realized that the warmth was from the blood that was inside of it. The big man had a bad cut on his upper, right arm.

"If you have a first aid kit, I can get that fixed up for you," Robert offered.

"I'll fetch it," Weston said and scampered away, disappearing from Robert's sight as he rounded the corner of the yacht's central cabin structure.

"You got a name?" the big man asked.

"I'm Dr. Robert Cline," he answered.

"You can call me Skipper," the big man told him. "Everyone else does."

"This is your boat?" Robert looked around. The *Lady Freedom* appeared to be a luxury boat. She was about half the size that the *TK* had been and wasn't armed, at least that he could see.

The Skipper shook his head. "No. If you want to know the truth, we stole her. There wasn't any other choice. We had to get out on the loch or. . ."

"The dead would have eaten you," Robert finished for him.

"Exactly," Skipper frowned. "There's a lot of that going around these days. The entire world has gone to hell."

Skipper led him into the *Lady Freedom*'s main cabin. There were three other people inside of it.

One was a tall, thin blonde, dressed in the tattered rags of what once must have been an expensive party dress. Her eyes were red from tears and she glared at him as they entered. Beside her sat a lady with jet black hair, who looked tough as nails. She wore a heavy coat and farm boots. Her hands were resting on a shotgun that lay across her knees. And lastly there was an older man that looked to be in his seventies with a long, gray beard and a cap atop his head.

Pulling out a chair at the room's central table, Skipper took a seat there, motioning for Robert to sit next to him. He held out his arm towards Robert as Weston came and handed the doctor the first aid kit he'd gone to get. Robert took it, placing it on the top of the table. He opened it and went to work cleaning Skipper's wound and getting it bandaged up. Not a single soul spoke. Robert felt their questioning gazes on him. It made him nervous.

"People," Skipper said all at once breaking the silence so suddenly that Robert couldn't help but flinch at the sound of his booming voice. "This is Dr. Robert Cline. Why don't you tell him who you are?"

"I'm Saul," the old man said. "Skipper there saved my arse on the dock. Apparently, we'd both had the same idea of stealing a boat and getting out on the water. If he hadn't come along, bashing in the heads of dead folks with the biggest bloody wrench I've ever seen, I'd be in their stomachs right now."

"Marian," the blonde spoke up next. "That's my name. My boyfriend and I were throwing a party on his boat when the dead came aboard and started eating everyone. None of us had a clue just how bad things had gotten on the shore. We'd been out on the loch for a few days and had only docked so that we could go into town for more supplies the next day when the dead found us. I escaped in a lifeboat. The Skipper picked me up. Been with him ever since."

Instead of introducing herself like the others had, the black-haired woman just continued to stare at him with an anger that he hoped wasn't really directed at him burning in her eyes.

"That's Valerie," the Skipper gestured at her. "She doesn't talk much but trust me, she can hold her own. Valerie has been with me since near the start. Found her on a farm not too far from the loch. She had shown mercy to her father when he rose up. Killed all the dead that had overrun the place too. Sometimes, I'll be honest, she scares the hell out of me but Valerie hasn't let me down yet."

Skipper paused, clearing his throat, "And you've met Weston."

Robert looked around at all of them again, such a motley, strange group to have come together but somehow they had, and they had survived where so many others hadn't.

"It's your turn now, doc," Skipper told him. "Who exactly are you to be out here on a military boat and just what the hell were you and your people up to?"

Wondering why he still felt the need to keep the nature of his mission to himself, Robert shrugged, "Not much I can say really. It's all classified."

Weston laughed so hard, he bumped into the table. The others were laughing too. Even the stoic, dark haired girl, Valerie was grinning.

"You serious, mate?" Weston fought to catch his breath between bursts of laughter.

"Enough!" Skipper roared, slapping a heavy hand, open palmed, onto the top of the table. Everyone's laughter went silent.

The Skipper turned in his seat to stare at Robert. "Don't you get it, man? There's no one left to keep your secrets from. We're no threat to you or whatever you're up to. I was a fragging fisherman before the world went to hell. Saul was the same though he had retired. Weston and Valerie are just kids, man. And Marian, well, look at her, doctor!"

Robert breathed a deep breath. He had to admit that the big man made a convincing argument.

"I guess you're right," Robert said after a moment.

"You bloody well know we are," Weston said.

"So who are you, doctor? I mean, really. And what were you doing out here on the loch in a boat like that one?" the Skipper asked.

"I'm a member of the Order," Robert answered. "And I am here because I am trying to save what's left of the human race."

"Come again?" Saul stared at him.

"What the frag is the Order?" Weston leaned over the table closer to him.

"Give him some space," the Skipper barked and Weston moved back.

"The Order is a top secret, multi-national organization that monitors and polices the supernatural. We deal with the threats that governments and militaries can't," Robert explained.

"You're screwing with us, mate," Weston blurted out.

"Weston, shut up and let the man talk," Saul urged.

"The Order has been around a long time," Robert went on. "We've kept this world safe for decades but this thing with the dead. . . it caught us as unprepared as everyone else. We weren't ready for it. The number of the dead out there kept growing beyond our ability to combat. The elder members of the Order knew our only hope was to find a means of curing whatever virus was returning the dead to life. You have to understand too that the Order doesn't just use science either. Among our ranks are the world's only real mages and the world's most powerful psionicists."

Before Robert could say anything more, it was the Skipper himself that interrupted him this time, stopping him. "Hold it right there. Did I just hear you say mages? You mean like bloody wizards?"

Robert nodded. "Magic, like in the fairy tales you heard as a kid, is real. It's just a lot more rare and more dangerous to use than in those stories."

"Uh huh," the Skipper said, an expression of clear disbelief on his face.

"Hey," Saul cut in. "What in the hell is a psion or whatever you bloody well just said?"

"Psionicists are like mages but they don't use magic. Rather they use their own inner strength or force of will to affect the world around them. The most common types of psionicists are telekinetics, telepaths, and clairvoyants," Robert hoped that at least of the group had heard the terms he was using.

Weston certainly had. "That's freaking wicked, mate!"

"Getting back to why the Order sent me out here," Robert said, "I'm after the Loch Ness Monster."

The room fell silent, everyone staring at him like he had lost his mind all over again.

"Are you seriously telling me that you think Nessie is real too?" The Skipper was leaning back in his chair now, arms crossed over his chest, a smug expression on his face.

"I can assure you no one in the Order refers to the monster as Nessie." Robert shook his head. "The creature in this loch is likely much older than the human race. . . and powerful too. It's not something you want angry at you, trust me on that."

"But why would you be hunting for the monster now?" Saul

asked. "It's the dead that are rising and eating the living, I mean, what the hell does the monster have to do with that?"

"There are those in the Order, myself included as its chief medical researcher, that believe the monster's blood may be the only hope we have of creating a cure for the virus that is causing the dead to rise up," Robert said.

Valerie spoke up for the first time. "How could you know that?"

"Once, the Order had a sample of the monster's blood. It's been lost over the years but our records show that it had off the charts regenerative properties," Robert said. "And frankly, it's what our mages and PSIs thought was the answer too."

Skipper was shaking his head, almost violently. "Mr. Cline, that's the most insane load of crap I have ever heard."

"Is it?" Saul defended the doctor. "Six months ago, would you have believed the dead could walk? I know I sure as hell wouldn't have."

"Me either," Weston agreed.

Looking at the big man, Robert had a flash of insight. He didn't think it was so much that Skipper didn't believe him but that he didn't want to put his yacht at risk. If Skipper accepted his story straight up, then the big man had to know that he was going to ask him for help. Skipper didn't want to risk what little they all had by going chasing after a monster.

"Okay," Skipper huffed. "That's enough of all this for tonight. I want you all to get some rest. Tomorrow isn't going to be any easier than yesterday."

"Hold on now . . ." Saul started but the Skipper gave him a look that shut the old man up quick.

"In the morning," the big man told them all again, his voice gruff and hard then turned to Robert. "Doctor, if you'll come with me. I have something I want you to see."

The big man led Robert back out onto the *Lady Freedom*'s main deck. They stood in the blowing snow on her bow, staring out at the shores of the loch, which seemed very far away to Robert. . . and he was glad of it. There was pretty much no chance of the dead reaching them out here, this far out on the water.

"Dr. Cline," the big man said, "that was one hell of a story you told in there, dangerous too."

Robert turned his head to glance at the Skipper. "Is that so?"

"We both know it is," Skipper spat over the side of the Yacht. "You were messing with their heads, doc, giving them hope that they can't afford to have."

"I was just answering the questions you asked me," Robert defended himself. "Nothing more."

"Be that as it might be, Dr. Cline. . .let's assume all that crap is true, which is something I ain't remotely sure of, then what comes next? You ask for our help finding this monster of yours, right? I didn't risk my arse saving those people in there just so you could come along and risk them all over again," the Skipper grumbled angrily.

"I get that," Robert nodded. "You don't want to risk what you have chasing something that might get all of us killed in the process and might not make a difference to the world at all even if we did somehow succeed but I, for one, am not ready to write the human race off as lost just yet. There's still hope if we can find the monster."

"From how you were mumbling about the monster when we dragged you out of the water, I'd say you found the thing once already and it kicked your arse," the big man snorted. "What's to say it won't kill you, and us with you, if you go after it again?"

Robert shrugged. He didn't have an answer to that.

"Besides, doc," the Skipper added, "this is a pleasure yacht, man. It ain't rigged up with the sort of gear you'd need to go hunting your monster anyway. Don't see any of your psychics or mages around either to lead you to it. Hell, we don't even have any weapons except for what we carried aboard with us and we are fragging low on ammo for those."

Thinking over what the big man had said for a moment, Robert smiled. "Maybe we can cut a deal then."

"What do you mean?" The Skipper frowned.

"You're low on ammo. Food and water too, I bet," Robert said.

"You know we are," the Skipper huffed.

"What if I knew where there was another boat that was just sitting there for the taking, a boat that was fueled up and ready to go?" Robert grinned.

The Skipper looked at him skeptically but seemed intrigued at least by what he was saying.

"There's another boat, like the one you picked me up from, nearby. It's a state of the art combat vessel, outfitted for eight people, with enough fuel to be operational for a couple of days. There would be rations, military weapons, and ammo aboard her too. . . not to mention the firepower to maybe be able to raid places along the shore for more supplies," Robert told the big man.

"I'd for sure be interested in that," Skipper admitted.

"Well, I could take you to her. She'd be all yours. I don't think there will be any more of my people from the Order coming to claim her." Robert watched the big man's expression closely. "She'd give you a hell of a lot better chance of surviving than this yacht you're on now."

"And in return you would want what? Us to go on a monster hunt with you?" The Skipper stared back at him.

"The boat is rigged with the best sonar available. She is completely geared up with everything we would need to find the monster in this loch so yeah, that would be the deal," Robert answered.

"Okay," the big man gave in. "You take us to this boat and I'll help you look for your monster for twenty-four hours. We don't find it by then, you agree to shut your mouth, and accept where you are now and what all of us are facing. That, I can agree to."

"Twenty-four hours?" Robert frowned. "That's not much time."

"That's my offer," the big man stood his ground. "Take it or leave it, doc."

****

Cato sat on the floor of the Temple's armory, catching his breath. Romona was pacing back and forth in front of the armory's locked door. She stopped abruptly, cursing, and smashed a gloved fist into it. Their charge for the hangar where the portal was had been cut short. They encountered a group of the dead too large for them to deal with on their own given that Romona was exhausted and her use of her telekinesis was limited.

"With all due respect, ma'am," Cato said, "you need to get some rest."

Romona spun around, glaring at him. Cato threw up his hands in a gesture of surrender.

"I just meant. . ." Cato started but she stopped him.

"I know what you meant, Cato," she told him. "It's just so fragging frustrating. Every minute that goes by, tens of thousands of people or more are dying out there beyond these walls."

"You banging your head against that door isn't going to change that, ma'am," Cato kept his voice calm and level. "Just get some rest. Get your strength back and then maybe we can get out of here."

Romona's shoulders slumped in defeat. He could see that she knew he was right but just didn't want to admit it.

"Come on," Cato urged her. "The dead can't get in here through that blast door. We're safe for now and you really do need some rest, ma'am."

She came over and took a seat on the floor next to him,

leaning her back against the armory's wall.

"You're pretty wise for a kid," Romona grudgingly told him. "I have to give you that. I can see why the Order's elders were so fired up about you. I've read your file, ya know? They really thought you'd be something special once you learned how to control your powers."

"My powers?" Cato shrugged. "That's a joke. I don't really have any other than low level telepathy at best."

Romona laughed. "If you believe that kid, I take back what I said about you being wise. Why do you think they came and recruited you? It wasn't because of your combat skills or your academics, Cato, plenty of folks out there could equal you in those. I can promise you that."

"Maybe they're wrong," Cato protested. "The elders aren't any more perfect than we are. They've made mistakes too. Just look at the crap we're in now. How did they not see this coming and put a stop to it?"

"They weren't wrong about you, Cato," Romona said firmly. "I'm just a Telekinetic not a sensitive and I can feel the power bleeding out of you, kid."

"I asked you to stop calling me kid," Cato reminded her.

Romona actually smirked as she made an attempt at what passed for an apology for her. "That you did. Guess you've earned that much. . . Cato."

"Thanks," he smiled at her. Romona was as beautiful as she was lethal. Cato swallowed hard and tried not to dwell on that. It wouldn't do either of them any good. "How long do you need to get your power fully recharged?"

"A couple of hours of sleep," Romona shrugged. "At least. It's been a hell of a last few weeks."

"Okay," Cato said, "I'll take watch. You log some Zs and we'll go from there."

Romona chuckled. "I don't remember putting you in charge. I outrank you by a hell of a lot, ya know?"

"I didn't mean to. . ." Cato blurted out, worried that he had ticked Romona off again.

"Just messing with you, Cato," Romona flashed him a wry grin. "Wake me up in about three hours and we'll get moving again."

Cato nodded. "Yes, ma'am."

He watched her take off her jacket and fold it up to use as a pillow. Romona curled up on the floor of the armory and was asleep a lot faster than he could have been. He was too keyed up and not the veteran of crap like this that she was. Romona Romy had faced supernatural horrors as her day job for years and lived through it, he was basically a rookie who had barely seen any action in the field compared to her.

There wasn't really much point in him staying up to keep watch. The dead wouldn't be getting into the armory unless they suddenly got smart enough to hack the Temple's system or got their hands on some very high-powered explosives and the knowledge of how to use them. Cato leaned his head back onto the wall and closed his eyes, thinking about the mess they were in. Fighting their way out of the armory wouldn't be too hard once Romona's telekinesis was recharged. Making it to the portal in the hangar wasn't an impossible thing either. The question that haunted him was what were they going to do then? Romona said the portal was supposed to open to somewhere close to Loch Ness where Dr. Cline's team had been sent to but that didn't mean that it did. The portal could lead to anywhere if the guys who opened it had screwed up somehow. They could find themselves leaping out of the frying pan into the fire, especially if the portal opened into a major city. Those were all overrun and fully belonged to legions upon legions of the hungry dead. Even with the gear they were looting from the armory and their powers, they wouldn't stand a chance in a place like that. What else could they do though? Forget about the portal in the hangar, maybe steal some sort of vehicle, fight their way out of the Temple, and find somewhere to hold up? Even if they did that, what kind of life would that be. . .the two of them alone? There certainly wouldn't be any help coming and eventually the dead would find them wherever they ran to. Trying to find Dr. Cline's group and helping them save the world made the most sense, that Cato had to attempt. It was what Romona was planning and she was the senior agent. The call should be hers but he had his doubts that it was the right one to make, not that he could think of any better options.

The minutes while Romona slept passed like hours. Cato stared at the walls and ceiling, alone with his thoughts. Part of him wanted to reach out with his telepathy and scan the Temple for other survivors. The memory of what had happened the last he'd tried stopped him though. Touching the mind of a reanimated dead person wasn't something he ever wanted to experience again. Cato looked at his watch and saw that it was finally time to wake Romona up. He shoved himself up onto his feet and stretched out his muscles. Unlike the door to his quarters had been, the door to the armory was so thick that the sound of the dead who were surely outside it, trying to force their way in, couldn't be heard. Cato sighed. His head hurt with a dull throbbing pain that he wrote off to be his own state of exhaustion.

Cato took a knee in front of where Romona lay curled up and reached out to gently shake her. As soon as the tips of his fingers made contact with her body, Romona's eyes flew open. An invisible force caught hold of Cato, lifting him from the floor, and hurled him across the armory. He crashed into its far wall with a loud thud. The breath was knocked out of his lungs in a pained grunt. Cato bounced off the wall, landing sprawled and hurting.

Romona leaped up, rushing over to him. "Cato!" he heard her shout.

Looking up at her, Cato saw the concern and guilt in her eyes.

"Was just trying to. . .wake you up," he muttered.

"Yeah," Romona took his head in her hands, "I'm sorry about that. I was having a nightmare I guess. When you touched me. . ."

"It's okay," Cato said, "I'm okay. I don't think anything's broken but I bet I am going to have one hell of a bruise."

Romona laughed. "Come on then. Let's get you up."

She helped Cato onto his feet and steadied him for a second until he found his own balance.

"That was one hell of a punch," Cato commented, rubbing at his aching back.

"You should be thankful that I didn't kill you," Romona told him and he saw that she was serious.

"Right," Cato nodded. "On the upside, your telekinesis seems to be fully recharged and ready to go."

Romoma chuckled. "I feel better too. I guess I needed some sleep more than I thought. Thanks for making me get some."

"I couldn't make you do anything you didn't want to, ma'am," Cato said and meant it.

Looking past him at the armory's blast door, Romona's expression of mirth changed into something more grim. "Guess we better get to it then. Grab whatever you're planning on taking with us and be ready for all hell to break loose when I open that door."

"Yes, ma'am," Cato nodded. They both had loaded up backpacks full of weapons and extra ammo. He slung a Vector machine gun over his shoulder by its strap and hefted an automatic shotgun, readying it. There were pistols holstered on each of his hips.

Romona was heavily armed too. She had a katana strapped to her back beneath her pack with handguns like his on her belt too. Her weapon of choice for use when she opened the door was a Vulcan M134 Minigun. The thing was a beast, weighing in at eighty-five pounds. Cato knew Romona had to use her telekinesis to help steady the weapon as she aimed its barrel towards the armory's door. The minigun was capable of firing six thousand, high powered rounds a minute. It was fed by a "disintegrating" belt of several hundred rounds. Romona wasn't planning on bringing the monster of a gun with them. Her intent was just to use it to clear the way once the door was opened. God only knew how many of the dead were waiting outside the armory for them.

"You ready?" Romona asked.

"As I will ever be," Cato quipped.

The M134 Vulcan's barrels were already beginning to spin as Romoma telekinetically grasped the armory's door and yanked it out of its frame. The door flew off to the right as dozens of the dead who had been pressed up against it by those behind them tumbled into the armory. The rest of the dead surged forward over those unlucky few, trampling them where they had fallen. The minigun roared as Romona hosed the creatures with a continuous stream of fire. The high powered rounds literally blew the dead apart, splattering their black blood and entrails in every direction, ripping through one then another. Romoma didn't let up. She kept the barrels of the minigun spinning. None of the dead were left standing when the minigun did finally fall silent.

"Frag," Cato muttered, looking around in disgust and astonishment at the gore that was everywhere.

"Time to move," Romona barked at him.

The floor was slick with black blood and entrails as Cato followed her out of the Temple's armory. Both of them were careful to avoid any heads that were in their path, giving them a wide berth. The minigun had torn up the dead but not killed all of them. A severed head was just as dangerous as an intact, reanimated corpse if you were dumb enough to let it bite you.

Leaving the armory behind, they raced along the corridor in the direction of the closest elevator. They were still a level above the hangar bay where the portal was located. Cato could feel the dull throbbing of the amount of psionic energy around it in his head. It was like a mild headache, painful and annoying.

All of the Temple's systems continued to be operational as best they could tell. Main power was still on and there had been no switch to the base's backup generators or the lights in the corridor would have been red and flickering, not the steady bright yellow-white that they were.

A dead man roared as he came rushing out of a side door along the corridor at Romona. She whipped a hand up in his direction, stopping the dead man with her telekinesis, and then flung him into the corridor wall, face first. Black gore flew into the air from the force of his impact. His body toppled onto the floor and didn't get up. Romona kept running the entire time with

Cato doing his dangest to stay right on her heels.

As the elevator came into view ahead of them, Romona hit the button on its control panel to open its doors while they were still yards away from it. Cato was glad she did. Three of the dead stumbled out of the elevator, apparently having been trapped inside of it. Their hollow eyes fell upon the two of them as the creatures snarled and moaned. Cato's automatic shotgun boomed in rapid succession as he headshot all three of the monsters. Fragments of skull bones and chunks of decaying brain matter exploded into the air as the creatures dropped one by one.

Romona reached the elevator first, jumping over the corpses of the dead in front of its doors. Cato rushed in right behind her. The elevator doors hissed closed in his wake and it began to descend.

"I kind of wish we could have brought that minigun with us," Cato commented as he ejected his automatic shotgun's magazine and loaded a fresh one.

"Quiet," Romona snapped at him. "We need to stay focused on what we're doing."

The elevator came to a stop and its doors slid open to reveal a mass of dead people in front of them.

"Oh crap!" Cato yelled, bringing his shotgun to bear on the

monsters.   Before he could get off a shot though, Romona screamed, shoving both of her hands forward.   A wave of telekinetic force exploded out through the doors of the elevator into the ranks of the dead.   It reduced the dead closest to the elevator to pulp and sent those behind them flying backwards, knocked off their feet, like the shockwave from a detonating grenade.   Romona wasted no time, sprinting through the elevator's doors and into the corridor, slowing only long enough to draw the katana sheathed on her back.   Some of the dead were staggering onto their feet but Cato didn't have a clear shot at the creatures because of Romona.   The woman seemed determined to slay all of the dead on her own.   Her katana slashed through the air, hacking into one skull only to be jerked free to strike again, taking the head off another.

Romona had the corridor directly outside the elevator totally cleared of the dead in less than two minutes.   Cato could hear more of the dead on their way though.   Their footsteps echoed through the Temple's corridors, coming from both directions.

"This way," Romona shouted at him and rushed forward, straight ahead towards the heavy blast doors that were blocking the entrance into the hangar.   Cato didn't have a freaking clue how they were going to get through them.

****

The snow had stopped as the sun rose over the frigid waters of Loch Ness. Robert steepled his fingers together, blowing warm breath inbetween his hands in an effort to warm them. Much to his surprise, he'd been able to get some sleep. He felt worlds better for it which was a good thing considering the day that lay ahead for everyone aboard the *Lady Freedom*. Robert had cut a deal with Skipper though it wasn't one that he was entirely happy with. Still, there hadn't been any other choice. This was the Skipper's yacht and if he was being honest with himself, Robert knew he needed the help of the big man and his people.

"Beautiful, isn't it?" a feminine voice said from behind where he was standing.

Robert turned, seeing that it belonged to Marian. She was bundled up in a thick coat and had come outside too to enjoy the rising sun.

"Yeah," Robert said quietly, nodding. "It is."

"I guess there are still some good things left in this world after all," Marian commented.

"You're up early," was all he could think to say back to her.

"Didn't sleep well," Marian frowned. "But then who does

these days?"

Robert shrugged. "Are the others awake?"

"Most of them." Marian stepped closer to him. "Valerie is getting breakfast ready. Saul and the Skipper have their guns taken apart on the table in there. I think they're cleaning them."

"You didn't come out here just to see the sunrise, did you?" Robert asked.

"I did but standing here with you. . . I was wondering. . ." Marian nervously stammered.

"Wondering what?" Robert pressed her.

"Do you really think you can save the world by finding this monster?" Marian finally managed to get out.

"I do," Robert told her.

"I just don't see how," Marian frowned. "I mean even if you find it and you somehow get this thing's blood, isn't it way too late for a vaccine to mean anything?"

Robert thought about what she said. So much of the world was dead already.

"A vaccine will save those of us who aren't infected. That's something I think is worth fighting for. It'll give us a starting point on the road back to how the world once was," Robert shrugged, wishing there had been a better answer he could have given her.

Marian looked like she was going to say something more but the Skipper's deep voice called out to them from the *Lady Freedom's* main cabin.

"Yo, doc!" the big man shouted. "We need you in here."

"Go on," Marian told him, her expression still sad and devoid of anything resembling hope.

Robert entered the cabin as the Skipper held the door open for him. If Weston had been asleep when Marian came outside, he was up now. He, Saul, and Valerie all sat around the table in the center of the room. There was a map of the loch rolled out across its top.

"About time you decided to show up," Weston grumbled.

Letting the kid's remark slide, Robert took a seat with the others. The Skipper did too. The big man cocked his head to one side, popping his neck. He looked utterly stressed. Robert didn't blame him for being that way. The big man had a lot riding on his shoulders. The way he saw things, everyone else on the *Lady Freedom* was depending on him to keep them alive.

"Dr. Cline and I have come to an arrangement," Skipper told the others.

"Let me guess, we're going to help him hunt down the Loch Ness Monster," Weston grinned.

Where the kid had seemed eager to believe him last night,

there was a different air about Weston this morning. Robert could see he was going to be trouble.

The Skipper nodded. "Yes, we are and in trade for our help, Dr. Cline is going to show us where to find a better boat than the one we've got that's loaded with the supplies to keep us going for a while longer. All we'll have to do is pull alongside it where the boat is docked and it should be ours for the taking according to the doc."

"Another boat? Really?" Saul got excited about that. "Military too, right?"

"She's called *The Thunder*," Robert said. "And yes, she's a torpedo boat, eighty feet-ish long, stocked with weapons, food, and water and enough onboard fuel to last a few days. She was supposed to be part of the Order's effort here to locate the monster in this loch. When my group arrived though, her crew and the soldiers that were supposed to be with her were all . . . gone. My group and I took her sister boat, the *TK*, which was waiting with her. We left *The Thunder* here," Robert stabbed at where the dock was on the map. "And she should still be there unless the dead have suddenly gotten a hell of a lot smarter."

"And what is it you're asking of us in trade for this information?" Saul asked.

"Just like the Skipper told you, I want your help in

completing my mission," Robert answered.

"I've agreed to Dr. Cline's terms in a limited sense," the Skipper announced.

"What? Without talking to us first?" Saul sounded shocked. "I thought we were all in this together?"

"We are but this isn't a democracy, Saul. It can't be if we're going to survive," the Skipper said. "I've kept us all alive so far, haven't I?"

"Sure, man," Weston nodded. "If you think this is the best way to go, then I'm in."

Saul and Valerie continued to look much more doubtful.

"I can't argue with you on you keeping us alive, Skip, but . . ." the old man frowned.

"It's just stupid," Valerie spoke up, taking everyone at the table by surprise.

"Excuse me?" The Skipper stared at the girl.

"You heard me, Phillip," Valerie said, calling the big man by his real name. "It's a waste of time and resources that we don't have to spare even if we are able to get this new boat the doc is offering."

"Finding the monster is the best hope we all have of getting through this mess." Robert was glaring at Valerie, hating her for seemingly not understanding just how much was on the line for everyone left alive in the world, not just their little group.

"I've heard what you've got to say about all that, Dr. Cline," Valerie glared back at him. "I just don't buy it."

"Enough," the Skipper clapped his hands together. "We've made it this far by sticking together and staying focused . . . That's what we're going to do now too. Dr. Cline is going to take us to *The Thunder* and in trade we're going to help him hunt for the monster for twenty-four hours, no more, no less. If we find the thing, we'll go from there, if not then *The Thunder* is ours and we'll have a much better chance of staying alive than we do now."

Valerie's cheeks were flushed red with anger and she looked ready to go off on anyone dumb enough to give her a chance to do so but kept her mouth shut.

"It's settled," the Skipper said again as if to remind them all one more time that he was in charge of things aboard the *Lady Freedom*. "Now, let's settle down and get to work. Dr. Cline has just showed us where *The Thunder* is docked but that doesn't mean taking her will be as easy as he thinks. She could have the dead aboard her by now. We need a plan on how to clear the bastards out if they're there."

****

Cato watched as Romona struggled with the blast door that led into the hangar where the portal had been opened. It made him wonder how the dead managed to get out to rampage through the Temple. Had they gotten out before the Temple's systems decided a lockdown was needed or were there other ways out of the hangar? Cato was new to the Order and hadn't really sat down and studied the layout of the Temple in depth. He supposed it didn't matter. There was nothing he could do to help Romona. Even her codes hadn't been able to get the door to open due to the locked down state the Temple was in. They had worked for other doors just fine but not the hangar.

"Arrggh!" Romona wailed, straining with all her might, as the heavy blast door trembled and shook in its frame as the invisible force of her telekinesis tugged at it. Veins bulgded on her forehead and her face was flushed red from exertion. Romona screamed again and finally wrenched the door free.

She threw herself out of its way as it thudded onto the floor where she had been standing.

The barrel of Cato's automatic shotgun was leveled at anything that might come bursting out from behind the door but nothing did. He had figured the hangar would be filled with the hungry dead. It wasn't. Its interior lights weren't functional and neither were their backups. The hangar would have been pitch black dark if not for the portal. It was in the center of the hangar, a bright glowing circle of bright blue that illuminated the corpses that were scattered all over the floor. Some of them were dead that had entered the Temple through the portal, the others were members of the Order who had died trying to stop them and had either been shown mercy or were too damaged by the dead to reanimate.

Seeing that the hangar looked to be clear, Cato rushed to Romona's side just in time to catch her as she collapsed. Ripping open the blast door had taken everything she had out of her. She was on the verge of passing out.

"You did it," Cato told her. "That was impressive as. . ."

"Shut up," Romona croaked. "Just get us through that thing to its other side."

"Yes, ma'am," Cato laughed, hefting one of her arms over his shoulders so that he could help support her weight as they made their way across the hangar. He kept his automatic shotgun ready in his other hand, watching the shadows for any signs of the dead.

Cato froze in his tracks as he noticed that the interior lights of a nearby armored personnel carrier were on and something, or someone, was moving around inside of it. He nearly opened fire as the side door of the A.P.C. slid open and a woman dressed in

Temple combat armor leaped out of it.

"Agent Cato?" the woman gawked at him in disbelief that matched his own expression as he recognized her.

"Murphy?" he yelped. "I nearly blew you to hell."

Three more people emerged from the A.P.C. after her. Two of them were army soldiers and not members of the Order. The last was a man he recognized as Agent Engler.

"Fragging glad you didn't, kid," Murphy told him. "What the hell are you doing here?"

Cato nodded in the direction of the portal, "We were on our way to go through that."

"Got to admit, we had considered doing that ourselves," Murphy admitted. "We retreated into that A.P.C. when the dead overran the hangar and it was lost. Been there trying to decide what to do next ever since."

Agent Engler was shaking his head. "Dang kid, I can't believe you're alive."

"Frag you, Engler," Cato said.

Romona's head had been down, hanging almost limply, staring at the floor. She raised it now. "Murphy, Engler, we're going through that portal and you're going with us."

Both Murphy and Engler's eyes went wide as they realized exactly who Cato was carrying along with him.

"Lt. Commander Romy," Murphy breathed. "You made it too."

"I did," Romona said, "thanks to this kid. We made it together. Now listen, we need to get out of the Temple and get to somewhere we can do something about all this zombie crap. That portal is the only way and we're all going the frag through it."

"We don't know where it goes to," Murphy said. "That's the only reason we haven't already."

"You weren't here when it was opened?" Cato asked.

"No," Engler answered. "We came in with the defense force trying to hold back the dead after things went to hell in here."

"It doesn't fragging matter!" Romona snapped. "It's supposed to open to somewhere close to Loch Ness where Dr. Cline's team is and that's where we're going. Do I make myself clear?"

Romona was the ranking member of the Order present, maybe even left alive altogether. It was her call and the others knew it.

"Ma'am, I don't think. . ." one of the two soldiers that had been hunkered down in the A.P.C. with Murphy and Engler started.

"I didn't ask you, soldier," Romona growled. "Your orders were to provide whatever support you could to the Order's operations were they not?"

"Well, yes ma'am but. . ." the soldier stammered.

"They haven't changed soldier and we're going to likely need every person with a gun we've got with us when we go through that portal. Whether you like it or not, whether you want to accept it or not, I am the ranking member of the Order here and I am telling you that you and your friend there are going with us."

The soldier shut his mouth.

"Yes, ma'am," his buddy said. "We're with you."

"Good," Romona spat a mouthful of blood onto the floor. Tearing down the blast door of the hangar had done more than just wear her out, Cato realized it had hurt her too.

They all approached the brightly glowing psionic doorway that led to somewhere beyond the walls of the Temple.

****

"We are so fragged," Weston spat into the water of the loch.

Robert lowered the pair of binoculars that the Skipper was letting him use. He didn't need to use them to see the great mass of the dead prowling about *The Thunder* where she was docked. The binoculars had just let him get a better look at the creatures. Robert wanted to argue with Weston but couldn't. The kid was right. They had all figured the dock would be clear of the dead by now or at worst only have a few of the things around it. No one had expected the mass that would be waiting on them.

"What are we going to do now?" Marian whimpered.

Everyone aboard the *Lady Freedom* was on her deck this morning. Valerie had traded the shotgun she normally lugged around with her for a high-powered hunting rifle and was watching the dead too through its scope.

"We have to get that boat," Saul said so loudly that Marian flinched, yanking her jacket tighter about her in the cold, morning air.

"Yeah, we do," Skipper said firmly. As much as the big man had put on a front about not really needing to get the torpedo boat, he was wanting it just as badly as Robert was now. The supplies aboard the *Lady Freedom* were sorely limited and being consumed quickly because of the number of folks aboard her. Robert had become the sixth mouth that the big man had to feed. Skipper wasn't the sort not to help someone if he could, no matter how much it cost him. *The Thunder* might not have that much space aboard it for supplies but both of them knew that what space it did have was likely still fully stocked. It would buy the Skipper and his people a few more days and in the hell that the world had turned into, every day was priceless.

"We can still do this," Valerie spoke up, taking everyone by surprise. The farm girl rarely spoke at all. They all turned to stare at her.

"We have very little ammo," the Skipper reminded her.

Valerie shrugged. "We won't need much."

"Okay," Weston marched over to her, almost getting in her face. "How we gonna do it then?"

"Think guys," she told them. "You've all had it fixed in your heads that we are just going to pilot the *Lady Freedom* up to that dock and board her. All you can think about is fighting your way through those things," Valerie paused and huffed, "use your heads. We don't have to go through them. All we have to do is lure them away from *The Thunder*.-1483973584 "

Robert blinked. He felt like an utter idiot. Valerie was right. He cursed himself for not seeing such a simple solution himself though of course it had risks too. Someone was going to be stuck with the job of luring the dead away and whoever did it might not make it back. . . and that person couldn't be him which meant he would have to live with the guilt if the dead did get whoever ended up doing it.

"You volunteering, girl?" the Skipper asked in a gruff voice. "You're right, we can get the boat that way without all of us being put at risk but. . ."

"I am if that's what it takes," Valerie answered the big man firmly. "I've thought a lot about what Dr. Cline is trying to do and how important it really is. If we can give him a chance at succeeding, it's worth all our lives and more."

"Speak for yourself, you. . ." Weston snapped but Saul slapped him on the back stopping him from finishing what he was saying.

Weston spun on the old man. "What the hell, man?"

"Stow it, Weston. . . unless you want to be the one I send out there," the Skipper ordered.

"I can't ask any of you to do this," Robert said. "This is my job to get done, not any of yours."

"I don't want to hear that crap either, doc," the Skipper grumbled. "Like it or not, when we picked you up and saved your arse, it became our job too."

Robert nodded, there was nothing else he could do. As much as he owed the big man and his people, finding the monster in the loch was the only hope for the entire world.

"Don't you dare think you're going ashore to draw those things away," Saul said. "You're going to be needed here to drive that boat and you fragging well know it. None of us have a chance in hell of doing that like you could. Valerie and I will go. She's the one with the brains to pull this off and hell, I'm the oldest. I have the least to lose. My time's almost up anyway."

"Saul," the Skipper said like he was about to argue with the old man but then stopped. After a moment, instead he asked, "Okay then, what are you guys going to need from us?"

"This thing's life raft," Valerie answered. "And of course, we'll have to take some of the weapons and ammo with us."

The Skipper nodded. "Whatever you need, it's yours, kid."

An hour later, Valerie and Saul were in the life raft, loaded up with gear and a pack full of about a third of the *Lady Freedom*'s dwindling stash of food. The Skipper had insisted the two of them take some of the food in case they survived the dead but got cut off from making their way back aboard either of the boats. No one had complained, not even Weston. Using the raft's oars, the two of them paddled out, even farther away from the shoreline, with the *Lady Freedom* as their cover. If they had the time, Valerie would have demanded that her plan be put on hold until after the sun had set and the world gone dark. Sadly, that wasn't an option. . . not one that either the Skipper or Robert were willing to explore. They had to take *The Thunder* and get aboard her as soon as possible. Thankfully, storm clouds rolled in again from the south. Thick waves of heavy snow were pouring from the sky. It worked just as well in terms of keeping their little raft from being seen by the dead on the shore. Valerie and the old man paddled onward up the shoreline from the dock where *The Thunder* sat. Almost all the dead in the area appeared to be massed at the dock. They brought the raft ashore without issue, abandoning it quickly for the cover of the trees, leaving tracks in the snow that was already beginning to cover the ground. The dead were much too stupid to hunt their prey in such a manner so that didn't matter.

Valerie led the way through the trees with the old man following her. Both of them had their guns slung over their shoulders. Valerie had drawn her boot knife. She clutched it tightly in her right hand. Saul carried a crowbar. The plan was to avoid using their firearms until either there was no other choice or they reached a position that she was happy with. If they just started shooting now, where they were, not all of the dead at the dock might be drawn to them. There was no certainty of that happening anyway but the closer they got, the better chance there was of it.

A dead woman lumbered in their path, her hollow eyes falling on them. Before she could start snarling or moaning, the old man rushed forward, raising the crowbar in his hands. It swung through the air with all the force he could muster, smashing into the side of her head. The bone there made a sickening crunching noise as it caved inward. The woman staggered about a couple of steps and then crumbled onto the snow-covered ground.   She lay there with foul, black gore running out from the indentation in her head and her open mouth.

"That was fragging close," Saul whispered.

"Gonna be a lot worse," Valerie responded. "Come on."

They marched on for another half hour or so, being forced to deal with a few others of the dead as quietly as they could as the things stumbled onto them. Saul was trembling from more than the cold.   His eyes kept flitting about, watching for more movement in the trees around them. Valerie knew they weren't going to make it much closer to the dock. They were pushing their luck already. She came to an abrupt stop. The old man nearly walked straight into her before realizing and catching himself.

"Here?" he asked.

"I reckon it's gonna have to be," Valerie nodded.

Saul and the Skipper had cooked up some homemade fireworks, simple but extremely loud things. Valerie was carrying two of the three they had put together. The old man had the other. Valerie removed one of hers from the pocket of her coat, along with a cigarette lighter. Lighting its fuse, Valerie lobbed the firework as far away from herself as she could. Saul did the same with his. The two fireworks detonated seconds apart, their loud booms echoing through the woods. Valerie waited around twenty seconds, giving the dead time to start moving towards them, and then lit the last one. She tossed it in the direction of the dock.

"That should do it," Saul sighed. "Hope you're ready, Val."

Valerie had brought her shotgun, not the rifle she'd briefly borrowed from the Skipper aboard the *Lady Freedom*. She worked its pump, chambering a round, and looked over at Saul.

"Just try to keep up, old man," Valerie smirked at him. Her expression actually made Saul chuckle despite the dire situation the two of them were in. They could hear the dead coming, hundreds, maybe thousands, of screeching, wailing, hungry voices.

They had to stand their ground long enough to let the first of the dead reach and engage them. If they ran sooner, there was a chance the bulk of the dead wouldn't be drawn into the chase they were hoping for. They didn't have to wait more than a few seconds before the first of the dead could be seen through the trees, charging towards their position.

Saul had his rifle ready and it bucked against his shoulder as he squeezed its trigger. He dropped the lead creature, a dead man in blood-stained work coveralls, with a well aimed head shot. Valerie held her fire, waiting for the dead to get closer still, only then did she open up on them. Her shotgun thundered, blowing apart the head of a dead man in the torn remains of a police uniform. As soon as she and Saul had taken those two shots, Valerie and the old man whirled about and ran like hell.

They had succeeded in drawing the dead to them. That was all those still aboard the *Lady Freedom* needed. Now, all they had to do was survive any way that they could. She and Saul had talked about their plan for that. Valerie had lived on a small farm in the area with her father. She and her dad had managed to hold out for quite some time before enough of the dead showed up at once to overrun their farm. Her father had died defending the place to his last breath. Valerie was hoping, praying, that there were still other farms like theirs out there that had somehow escaped the notice of the dead. If there were, all they had to do was find one. Sure, it wouldn't be safe to stay there no matter how well stocked or fortified said farm might be but whoever was there would surely have a car or truck that they all could use to make a run for it. Valerie did her best to ignore the fact that there might not be anywhere left to run to.

Valerie and Saul sprinted through the woods around the loch. Saul cried out as one of his feet slipped in the snow and he toppled into the trunk of a tree. Its bark scraped away skin from his right cheek and his hands as Saul tried to catch himself. The old man flopped into the snow.

"Saul!" Valerie yelled but before she could start back to help him, the dead caught up to them.

Several of the dead rushed Saul. To his credit, the old man took out the first of the creatures with a point blank shot to its forehead. The fingers of a snarling dead woman closed around the rifle's barrel as she yanked it from the old man's hands. Saul was knocked backwards as a dead teenager plowed into him. Managing to draw his knife, Saul buried its blade in the side of the teenager's head, twisting it there. The dead young man went limp above Saul. The old man grunted as he shoved the dead kid off of him. The rotting woman who had taken his rifle dropped the weapon, lunging at him. . .and she wasn't alone. The half a dozen or so of the dead piled onto the old man. Saul was wailing, screaming in terror and pain as their teeth sunk into his flesh and their nails tore at his skin. Valerie watched helplessly, knowing Saul was already dead. She couldn't even get a shot at his head to stop the old man from turning if the dead left enough of him for that to happen. Tears welled up in Valerie's eyes but she had no time to cry. The dead were coming after her too.

Valerie ran, legs pumping beneath her, as fast as she could. Her shotgun boomed as she blew a one-armed, dead man out of her path. The heavy slug she fired opened a fist-sized hole in his chest and blew gore out of his back, sending the dead man reeling away just in time for her to rush past him.

All around her, Valerie could hear the shrieks of the hungry dead. The things were everywhere. She burst out of the woods on the bank of the loch. In the distance, she looked to see gunfire blazing from the direction of where *The Thunder* was docked. Clearly, she and Saul hadn't been able to lure away all of the dead but she hoped, prayed, they had done enough. Trapped between the freezing water and the dead, Valerie had nowhere left to run. The trees were full of glowing, yellow eyes burning in the darkness as they closed in on her. She had seen what the creatures had done to her father and to Saul. Valerie had no intention of letting them take her like that. Opening her mouth, Valerie shoved the barrel of her shotgun into it, squeezing the weapon's trigger. Her head exploded in a shower of red gore.

****

Cato stepped into the shimmering portal. The world around him blurred, distorting, bending. He was yanked forward, shifted through space and time, then everything flashed white. Cato was still moving forward when he emerged from the portal's other side. The ground crunched and was slick beneath his boots. He was walking on snow and the air around him was now freezing cold. Cato fell onto his knees, puking up the contents of his stomach. His vomit steamed where it lay in the snow. The others had come through the portal after him. All of them except for Romoma looked sick too. . . not that she was immune to the portal's effects. Cato could see that the journey through it had messed with her too just not as badly. Romona only appeared to be disoriented.

"Get up!" Romona barked. "People, we got incoming!"

Murphy, Engler, and the two soldiers with them stumbled onto their feet. Cato couldn't manage it though. Romona rushed to where he was, standing over him, to protect him. They had indeed leaped out of the frying pan, into the fire. Cato couldn't even guess at how many of the dead were in the woods. There were so many inhuman voices, shrieking and crying out in anger and hunger that it sounded like an army of the creatures were coming for them.

Suddenly, in the distance to the west, erupted the sound of gunfire, louder than even the cries of the dead. Somewhere in that direction a heavy machine gun was roaring. That meant there were other, living people nearby.

Corporal Hank, one of the two soldiers with them, opened fire with his M-16A as a squealing deader crashed out of the trees, charging towards him. Hank's bullets shredded the dead man's chest, stopping his forward momentum. It was a single, booming shot from Engler's .44 Magnum that put the creature down though. He had drawn it and gotten off the shot with the skill and speed of an old West gunfighter. Engler drew his other Magnum as more of the dead poured out of the woods.

Murphy was a geokinetic. She raised her hands upwards and the earth itself buckled under the feet of the dead. Rocks flew out of the ground like shrapnel from an explosion, ripping the dead creatures to pieces, severing arms, legs, and heads. Her quick action had stopped the first wave of the dead and bought them all some time. The group got moving, running like hell through the woods in the direction they heard the heavy machine gun still continuing to fire.

Romona was in the lead. Cato, Murphy, and Engler followed closely after her. The two soldiers with them fought a running battle behind them, firing into the ranks of the dead which poured from the woods in pursuit of them. It was a futile effort. Two rifles were far from enough to hold back the army of dead coming after the group.

"There!" Cato yelled, pointing as the loch came into view through the trees ahead of them. Upon its water sat a military boat with its deck gun blazing.

Aboard *The Thunder*, Dr. Robert Cline saw the group coming. Weston was manning the ship's machine gun, tearing the few dead creatures trying to storm the dock to shreds. Valerie and the old man had succeeded in luring the bulk of the dead away. He and Weston had boarded the torpedo boat without much trouble. The Skipper had covered them with sniper fire from the deck of the *Lady Freedom* as they leaped over from one boat to the other. Robert had dispatched a dead woman with a head shot from his Glock, her body toppling over, splashing into the water of the loch. Weston had brought a pump action shotgun with him. The kid blew a dead man to hell, finishing up clearing *The Thunder's* deck. He worked the shotgun's pump, chambering another round before seeing that it was going to take a lot more to deal with the crowd of rotters on the shore. While the old man and Valerie had drawn away hundreds if not thousands of the dead, there were still several dozen of the things not far from the dock where *The Thunder* was moored. Their gunfire had gotten the attention of the monsters and now they turned back toward the boat floating on the loch, their yellow eyes glowing. Almost as one, the creatures had rushed the dock. Weston tossed his shotgun aside, racing to one of the heavy machine guns on the torpedo boat's deck, bringing it to bear on the monsters. The kid was doing a hell of a job keeping the rotting bastards from reaching *The Thunder.*

Robert watched the group approaching the ship. He was supposed to be getting the torpedo boat underway but froze upon seeing them. From the combat armor they wore, it was easy to see that four of the group were agents of the Order of the Eternal Light. Help had shown up at last. . . assuming they could fight their way through to join himself and Weston aboard the boat.

"Hey!" Robert shouted at the kid but Weston couldn't hear him over the fire of the huge machine gun. Sprinting to his side, Robert grabbed Weston, getting his attention. "We got friendlies incoming! Cover them!"

"You got it!" Weston's head bobbed up and down as he shifted his line of fire, swinging the gun around to target the dead on the shore beyond the dock. High powered rounds ripped through the rotting bodies of the dead gathered there, blowing arms and legs off their bodies, sending black gore splashing through the air, and thinned out the dead who were between the approaching group and the dock.

"Go on!" Weston yelled at Robert, motioning for the doctor to get on with firing up *The Thunder*'s engines.

Robert hesitated, glancing at the shore. The group was getting closer. He wanted to be there to meet them when they came aboard but also knew that there were hundreds of hungry, rotting, dead folks on their heels. The choice of what to do was made for him.

As the group reached the end of the dock, one of the female agents turned as if to confront the charging mass of the dead, thrusting her hands outward, angled at the bank of the shore. The bank was lined with heavy rocks and boulders. Those near the edge of the dock started to explode, one by one, and even more astonishing than that, their shrapnel flew only towards the dead. A shard of rock tore through the face of a snarling man whose guts were dangling out of the open cavity of his abdomen. Another larger piece ripped the head of a dead woman completely from her shoulders in a spray of thick, black blood. The exploding rocks decimated the ranks of the dead.

"What the. . .?" Weston yelped, his fingers slipping away from the firing mechanism of the heavy machine gun. It fell silent as the young man gawked at what he'd just seen. Robert saw him getting ready to start shooting again but Weston had swung the machine gun about to target the approaching strangers. The doctor reached Weston just in time to keep him from opening fire on them.

"They're not. . . they can't be human," Weston stammered.

"They are," Robert assured the young man. "They're members of my Order!"

"Somebody get this fragging boat moving!" a hard looking, though beautiful woman barked as the group of strangers rushed aboard *The Thunder*.

"Yes, ma'am!" Specialist Andrews snapped, darting into *The Thunder*'s CIC. Seconds later, the torpedo boat revved to life.

"Careful!" Robert warned her. "We're still moored to the dock!"

The woman closed her eyes, appearing to concentrate. The thick ropes holding *The Thunder* to the dock snapped.

"Now we're not," the woman snapped back at him. "Andrews! Get us moving!"

Corporal Hank and the others continued pouring fire into the dead who had waded through the carnage of their brothers and sisters that had been pulped by the exploding rocks and were now racing across the dock towards *The Thunder*.

The torpedo boat shot forward, bouncing over the surface of the loch, leaving the dock behind. Corporal Hank whooped "Oorah!"

The woman, who was clearly in charge of the group, approached Robert and Weston where they were still standing at the .50 caliber machine gun with a younger agent at her side. The younger agent was intently staring at him.

"That's him, ma'am," the young agent said. "Dr. Robert

Cline, leader of the group dispatched to locate a cure for the virus that's reanimating the dead."

"You're a telepath," Robert met the young agent's eyes with his own and then turned his attention back to the woman. "And you must be Lt. Commander Romona Romy."

"I am and this is Agent Cato," Romona nodded. "It's dang good to meet you, doc."

"You as well," Robert grinned. "I was beginning to wonder if I was the only member of the Order that was left alive."

"Pretty close," Romona frowned. "The Temple was infiltrated and overrun. As far as we know, we're the only ones who got out."

"No. It can't be. . ." Robert muttered as her words sunk in.

"It is," Cato confirmed. "The dead got into the Temple through the portal that was used to bring you and your people here."

"Hey," Weston snapped at them all. "Anyone want to clue me in on what's happening here?"

"Who is the kid?" Romona asked.

"His name's Weston," Robert answered. "He's one of a group of survivors that saved my life."

"I see." Romona glanced over at the small yacht which was doing its best to keep pace with *The Thunder*. "That explains that then. Andrews! Slow us down and bring us to a full stop!"

The soldier answered her over the comm. piece in her ear as the roar of *The Thunder's* engine decreased and came to a stop in the water. The small, sporting yacht came up beside her.

A tall, muscular, burly man with a high powered hunting rifle in his hands stood on the yacht's deck. A thin blonde in the remains of what once was surely a very expensive and pretty dress stood behind him. She held a pistol in her right hand but it was held, barrel downward, towards the deck the woman stood on.

"Who the hell are you people?" the big man challenged Romona.

"I am Lt. Commander Romona Romy of the Order of the Eternal Light," she shouted back at him. "Dr. Cline, here, says that we're on the same side, sir, so I suggest you lower that rifle before I am forced to lower it for you."

"Skipper. Do as she says," Robert called out. "These people are here to help us."

The big man appeared to be royally ticked off at being told what to do by a woman while he was standing on the deck of his own boat. For a second, Robert thought the Skipper might do something really stupid and breathed a sigh of relief as the big man lowered his gun.

"You coming aboard?" Romona asked the Skipper.

The big man shook his head. "Nah, I don't think so. The way I see things, having two operational boats is a hell of a lot better than one."

Romona chuckled, "Man has a point. We'll have a much better chance of finding that monster of yours, Dr. Cline, with two boats."

****

The *Lady Freedom* and *The Thunder* sat side by side on the loch. The joint planning meeting of the Skipper's rag-tag band of survivors and those under Romona's command was held inside the *Lady Freedom*'s cabin. There was no threat of being attacked by the dead. The monsters weren't able to swim and the depth of the loch's water made it impossible for the creatures to come at the two boats from beneath them.

The Skipper, Marian, and Weston sat staring across the table in the center of the room at Lt. Commander Romona Romy and Agent Cato. Dr. Robert Cline sat in the middle between the two groups.

"That boat is supposed to be ours," the Skipper said, his voice cold and flat.

"The Thunder belongs to the Order of the Eternal Light," Romona countered. "It was brought out here to find the monster Dr. Cline is after. You have no legal claim to her."

"Legal," the big man huffed. "Ain't no such thing anymore, ma'am. Your man there gave us his word that she was ours if we got him to her."

Romona glanced at Dr. Cline.

"That's true," the doctor admitted, "but not without the condition of you and your people helping me search for the monster first."

"You did agree to that," Marian spoke up, eying the Skipper.

"That was before his people showed up out of the blue," the Skipper grumbled. "Look at them. They're better armed and prepared to deal with all this crap than we are by a long stretch."

"That doesn't matter," Romona argued.

"It damn well does to me," the Skipper roared, pounding a clenched fist onto the top of the table. "If they take that ship and leave us here. . . that's pretty much the same as murdering us. We've got barely any supplies and no real hope of finding any more without the kind of firepower support that boat can offer."

"No one is leaving anyone!" Robert shouted. "The only real hope any of us have is if we all work together and both of you dang well know it."

"Oh, I think we'd be just fine if we left this jerk right here and now," Romona countered.

"You fragging. . ." the Skipper started but Cato butted in before he could finish.

"The truth is . . ." Cato blurted out… "the truth is even if we give you *The Thunder*, that's not going to change anything in the long term. In a few days, you'll be right back where you are now, running out of food, fuel, and ammo all over again and you know it. Now let's stop all this bickering and get busy doing what really needs to be done."

"And that's finding this monster of yours?" Weston asked.

"I am sure Dr. Cline has told all of you that its blood may hold the key to curing the virus that has brought the dead back to life. If we can get a sample of that thing's blood, Dr. Cline should be able to engineer a means of stopping the dead once and for all. . . all of them."

"Yeah," Skipper grunted. "He told us. Told us a bunch of other crap too about people with powers and secret organizations. Not sure I believe any of it."

"I . . .I . . .I saw the other woman with them. . ." Weston stammered.

"Agent Murphy," Romona filled in her name.

"She blew up the rocks on the shore with her mind," Weston

said.

Skipper's head whipped around at the kid. "What the hell are you talking about?"

Romona raised a hand. "Stop. I can show you something that will convince you right now, Mr. Skipper."

The big man glared at her. "Is that so?"

She took her sidearm from its holster and held it out for him to take.

"What the . . .?" the big man balked. "I don't want your gun. What's that got to do with anything anyway?"

"Fine, use yours. I want you to shoot me in the head," Romona told him.

"You're crazy," Skipper gawked at Romona, shaking his head. "What is wrong with you people?"

"Nothing," Romona chuckled. "If you won't take out your gun and shoot me, I'll do it for you."

Skipper squirmed in his seat as the pistol on his hip flew out of its holster, rising up to hover above the table, aimed at Romona's forehead. The weapon fired. The shot was point blank but none the less, Romona didn't so much as flinch. The bullet met an invisible force between the two of them. The force stopped the bullet mid-flight and held it motionless in the air for everyone at the table to see.

"Whoa," Weston breathed in awe. "That's awesome."

Skipper swallowed hard. "Uh. . . okay then. Maybe there is some truth to all the craziness."

"Look, we've got to find that monster," Robert assured the big man. "Its blood is the only hope the world has left."

"Alright, doc," Skipper nodded. "I guess we're in."

"Great!" Robert smiled.

"How can we help?" Weston sincerely sounded eager to get involved.

"I don't know that you can," Romona frowned. "This isn't a game, kid."

"Two boats are better than one," Skipper reminded Romona.

Romona didn't say anything more to Skipper. She shifted in her seat to look at Robert. "Dr. Cline, just how hard is it going to be to find this thing?"

"Loch Ness is one of the deepest bodies of fresh water in Europe, not to mention, we're talking around twenty-three *miles* surface area," Robert shrugged. "There are reasons beyond the monster supposedly being a PSI as to why it's never really been found and trapped before."

"The Order spent a fortune on equipping *The TK* and *The Thunder* to find it," Romona said. "Are you telling me that all that sonar crap still won't be enough?"

"Not in the amount of time we have," Robert shook his head. "Every minute that goes by, the closer the human race gets to extinction. The faster we find the monster, the better. The gear that the Order invested in might get the job done but even if we were able to divide it between *The Thunder* and the *Lady Freedom*, with as much of an area we're dealing with, it could still take days or even weeks."

"Frag," Romona scowled.

"I don't get it," Weston said.

"Don't get what?" Robert asked.

"If your mates here are psychics, doc, why can't they just find this thing with their powers?" Weston suggested.

Out of the mouths of babes, Robert thought.

Robert looked at Romona. "Could we do that? Is it possible?"

"The Order has many types of PSIs at its disposal- Seers, Clairvoyants, Locators – but none of them have had much luck locating the monster over the years. That's why most in the Order believe it to have psionic abilities too so it can block them, shield itself from being detected," Romona explained. "But regardless, the Temple was lost, Dr. Cline. You know this. If there any of those types of PSIs left alive, they sure as hell aren't with us."

"You're telekinetic," Weston grinned at Romona. "Can you

do anything else?"

Romona shook her head. "No. That's my only talent."

"So what can the other people in your group do?" Weston pressed her.

"Agent Murphy is a powerful geokinetic," Romona answered.

"That's how she did that stuff at the dock, making those rocks on the shore attack the dead," Weston cut in.

"Yes," Romona nodded.

"But there are two more of you," Weston said. "What about them?"

"Agent Engler is a chronokinetic," Romona shrugged, frustrated with the teenager's questions.

"Whoa," Weston's mouth fell open.

"What now?" Skipper frowned.

"He can control time, making extremely limited jumps through it," Romona frowned. "At best, we're talking minutes. His talent won't help us find the monster."

"That's only three of you," Weston looked at Cato. "She hasn't mentioned you yet. What's your power?"

Cato appeared uncomfortable at being put on the spot in such a manner. He cleared his throat before answering, "Truth is, I don't really know."

"How the hell can you not know?" Skipper challenged him.

"Agent Cato was sought out and recruited by the Order because of the power we sensed inside of him," Romona answered for Cato. "Sometimes, we don't really know what our recruits are capable of until we get them into training and force them to push themselves. As for Agent Cato, so far, we've discovered he has the potential to be one of the most powerful telepaths we've ever encountered."

Cato's head whipped around to Romona.

"Yes, Cato," Romona told him, "you are that strong. You just haven't gotten your crap together yet in your head."

"Wow." Cato leaned back in his seat.

"And there's a chance you could be even more than that," Romona went on. "To be honest, we hadn't fully figured you out yet."

"Well, there you go then," Weston laughed. "If he's as powerful of a telepath as you think, can't he just tap into the monster's mind or whatever and find out where it's hiding?"

"It's not that easy," Romona shook her head again. "If the monster is as powerful of a PSI as the Order suspects, the thing could sense Agent Cato's attempt to do so and strike back against him."

"In other words, the thing could cook my mind inside of my

skull if I ticked it off," Cato said, sounding none too happy about that thought. "But, me trying might just be the only hope we have of finding the thing quickly."

Romona blinked, "Cato, I can't allow you to put yourself at risk like that. It'd be extremely risky for even a senior telepath. . . "

"Frankly, ma'am, it's not your call to make anymore," Cato shrugged. "The Order is just as lost as the rest of the world. The Temple has fallen. Any surviving agents left are scattered about, fighting for whatever time they can buy themselves before the dead finally get them. We're the only ones in a position to do something that could change that."

"You could die. . . or worse," Romona protested.

"We're all going to die if the dead aren't stopped," Robert said. "It's just a matter of time."

"I am not going to pretend I really understand any of the crap you people are going on about but if that guy . . ." Skipper pointed across the table at Cato, "...if he really has a shot at finding the monster fast, I'd say we all need him to try."

Romona grunted. Deep down, she knew they were right. Cato was their only hope. That didn't make it any easier for her to risk the life, the mind, of an agent who was under her command.

"Are you sure, Cato?" Romona asked. "This is not something I am going to order you to try. Hell, I don't even think you're ready to try something like this."

"I'm the only shot we've got," Cato answered.

"Uh, okay . . ." Weston said. "How does something like that work?"

"All you have to do is shut up and give me a minute," Cato told him.

"What? You're doing this right now? Right here?" Skipper asked.

"Why not?" Cato said.

"Everybody keep quiet and let him try," Romona ordered.

Everyone gathered around the table and the *Lady Freedom*'s main cabin fell silent as Cato closed his eyes.

****

Cato's hands clasped the edge of the table. His knuckles were white from the pressure of his grip on it. Part of him was terrified of what he was doing. His eyes were closed tight but it wasn't them he was using to see with. Cato lowered his mental defenses, shedding them layer by layer. With each passing second, he was more exposed and more vulnerable. At first, his mind brushed against those of the people gathered about the table with him. He could hear their thoughts and feel their own, personal fears. Cato bypassed them, expanding the reach of his telepath beyond the *Lady Freedom's* cabin, beyond her deck, and across the loch. He was careful not to establish any sort of contact with what passed for the minds of the dead. The last time that had happened, Cato had barely been able to pull himself free of the dead's darkness. The minds of the dead were like blackholes of all consuming hunger. Cato sensed the others of their group aboard *The Thunder*, and ignored them too. He had never tried something like this, of this scale, before. During the last hours he was at the Temple, Cato had swept it, looking for others still alive. That was a broad search in a sense and this one, while covering more distance, was much narrower. He was looking for only one mind, one stream of consciousness. . .and he had to find it.

There was nothing to be sensed on the surface of the loch. If the monster were indeed in its waters, the thing was far beneath them, hidden in their depths, just as so many had suspected over the years. Cato turned his focus downward to those depths, straining to find, to sense, the monster.

And then. . . he found it.

His mind met the monster's. The creature made no effort to

shut him out. Instead, it sucked his consciousness into its own. The monster's mind was utterly alien in its nature, impossible to comprehend. Its thoughts were like crashing waves of raw power that washed over him. Cato couldn't understand them but then he didn't need to. All he needed to do was figure out where the monster was. That was all.

A cold, inhuman voice spoke to him telepathically. Cato shivered in his seat at the table in the *Lady Freedom's* cabin.

"Human, I know what you and those with you seek and you shall not have it," the voice told him. "You don't need to find me. I am coming for you."

Cato sensed boiling rage and physical movement. He felt the monster stirring in the depths, darting out of the darkness of the cave where it had been slumbering. It was on the move now, racing upwards towards the surface of the loch, fully intent upon making sure they all died for coming after it, and that none of them escaped its fury.

Cato's eyes shot open in stark terror as his hands released the edges of the table and he screamed at the top of his lungs.

****

Skipper jumped out of his seat at the table as Cato thrashed about as if in some kind of seizure. Romona, who was sitting beside Cato, took hold of him in order prevent the younger agent from harming himself.

"Hold him!" Robert shouted at Romona.

Weston just sat watching it all in shock.

Cato's eyes popped open. The young agent had gone pale. His breath came in ragged gasps.

"It's coming!" Cato blurted out. "Right now!"

Robert's eyes cut to Romona.

"How could he know that?" Skipper growled.

"You idiot!" Weston snapped. "He's a telepath! Agent Cato was trying to find the thing, wasn't he? I'm guessing he found the creature and ticked it off."

"We need to get back aboard *The Thunder*," Robert told Romona.

The Lt. Commander nodded as Cato began to come fully around and seemed to get control of himself.

"Come on!" Cato yelled, leaping up from where Romona cradled him against her at the side of the cabin's table.

Everyone raced onto the deck of the *Lady Freedom*. Skipper and Weston were chasing after the members of the Order.

"What about us?" Skipper shouted.

"You're on your own for now," Romona barked. "Just get

this yacht moving and get the hell out of here!"

The big man clearly wasn't happy with her response. He'd been hoping to have some of *The Thunder*'s weaponry moved over aboard the *Lady Freedom*. There was no time for that now. If Agent Cato was to be believed, the monster in the loch could show up any second.

Romona ran for the edge of the *Lady Freedom*'s deck, leaping into the air. As she jumped, Romona picked up Robert and Cato, her telekinesis lifting all three of them and carrying them across the water between the yacht and the torpedo boat. They landed on the deck of *The Thunder* directly in front of Corporal Hank, who was staring, bug eyed, at them.

"Get this ship moving!" Romona ordered. "Now!"

Aboard the *Lady Freedom*, Skipper hurried to her bridge, firing up the yacht's engines. The *Lady Freedom* was already bouncing over the water of the loch's surface, speeding away, as *The Thunder* was still trying to get moving. Marian came running up behind him where he stood at the yacht's controls.

"What's going on?" Marian wailed.

"The monster!" Skipper yelled at her. "It's coming. Go find Weston. He's going to need your help!"

Marian darted from the *Lady Freedom's* bridge. She found Weston out on the deck. The kid was readying a small stack of weapons, one at a time, checking them and making sure they were loaded. He looked up and saw her coming.

"Here!" Weston tossed her a high powered, hunting rifle.

Marian caught it. She held the rifle tight.

"You really think these are going to matter against the Loch Ness Monster?" Marian asked Weston.

"They're all we've got," he sighed. "So they had better."

Neither of them really had any idea what to expect in terms of the monster. There were so many stories and legends about the thing, so many videos, fake or real, all over the internet before it went down after the dead rose. There were also an equal number of theories about what the monster was. The only things they had learned about the creature from the people from the Order of the Eternal Light were that the monster was indeed real and apparently the thing was psychic.

Aboard *The Thunder*, Dr. Robert Cline watched the *Lady Freedom* speeding away. He owed his life to Skipper and the others on her. Robert hoped that they were going to be okay. The *Lady Freedom* wasn't armed for war like *The Thunder* and she wasn't as fast either. The yacht was built for speed but not on the level that the torpedo boat was. Robert caught himself, grabbing onto the rail that ran around the main deck of *The Thunder* as the torpedo boat surged into motion. Its engines were howling. The torpedo boat shot forward in the opposite direction that the *Lady Freedom* had fled. Romona had hastily warned Corporal Hank and the others about the danger they were in.

Robert tore his gaze away from the water and stumbled towards the torpedo boat's CIC. Corporal Hank was yelling, "Action stations! Action stations!"

The corporal wasn't navy, he was army, but that hadn't stopped him from taking charge of things with the boat. Andrews was piloting *The Thunder* while Cato had recovered and had taken over its radar/sonar station. Agent Murphy was manning the torpedo boat's weapon console. Her powers were essentially useless on the water being a geokinetic. The bottom of the loch was far too deep for her powers to effect it in any way that would help on the surface.

Lt. Commander Romona Romy and Agent Engler remained on *The Thunder's* deck, taking gunner positions at the .50 caliber machine guns there. Romona readied the huge weapon she stood behind as the torpedo boat picked up even more speed.

"I've got a contact!" Cato called out. "It's CBDR and coming in fast, port side!"

Robert saw that the corporal looked panicked.

"That thing must be trying to ram us!" Corporal Hank blurted out. "Evasive maneuvers!"

"Yes, sir!" Andrews barked at *The Thunder's* helm.

The torpedo boat banked hard, changing course.

"The contact has altered course too!" Cato warned. "It's still CBDR."

Out on *The Thunder's* deck, Engler was manning the aft .50 caliber. Romona heard his voice over the comm. unit in her ear.

"Ma'am! We got trouble! Big fragging trouble!" Agent Engler cried out. "I've got visual contact on the monster. The thing is several hundred feet long!"

"Then bloody well open fire on it already!" Romona raged.

Agent Engler's .50 caliber roared to life as he held its firing mechanism tight. A continuous stream of rounds flew towards the approaching monster, splashing into the water of the loch. Agent Engler couldn't see that they were having any effect on the massive creature. Hell, he couldn't even tell if they were hitting it. Nonetheless, Agent Engler kept firing.

Inside *The Thunder's* bridge, Corporal Hank shouted, "Options?"

"This boat is rigged to deploy charges in its wake," Robert spoke up. "Could we use those?"

Corporal Hank glanced at Agent Murphy who was at the weapons console.

"I can do it," she said. "But the charges weren't meant to be deployed at this kind of speed. They could. . ."

"Just fragging do it," Corporal Hank ordered.

Agent Murphy scowled at the army corporal. She was outside of his chain of command and none too happy with him just taking things over. Still, Agent Murphy followed his order. "Deploying charges now."

The launcher on the rear of the torpedo boat swiveled around on its turret as *The Thunder's* sonar guided it, doing its best to lock onto the approaching monster, then began firing. It spat half a dozen charges, all only seconds apart, into the water ahead of the monster. The giant creature plowed straight into the first one. As it blew, Agent Cato cried out at the sonar console, almost doubling over in pain.

The giant monster was struck by a second charge before it could maneuver away. At the rear of the torpedo boat, where Agent Engler was manning the heavy machine gun there, he saw the detonations of the explosives. The monster was able to turn and avoid the other shots but the first two had certainly given it something to think about. He squinted, trying to see any sign of blood in the water but couldn't. Still, he knew the monster had to have been hurt by the hits it had taken.

Inside the bridge, Corporal Hank shouted, "What the hell is wrong with him?"

Andrews shook his head, clearly not having a clue. Murphy's lips spread into a smug grin though.

"Cato's a telepath," she answered. "I think he's feeling what that monster out there is feeling."

Corporal Hank didn't quite know what to make of her answer.

"Direct hits confirmed!" Cato said, having pulled himself back upright, a pained expression on his face. "In more ways than one. I. . . I can feel some of what that thing out there is feeling and if it wasn't ticked off before, it sure as hell is now."

"I'd say that's good cause for us to hit that bastard again." Corporal Hank's grin made Cato think of a feral cat.

"Trying," Cato told him, "but the monster has altered course. It's going after the *Lady Freedom.*-947101022 "

"Andrews, bring us about," Corporal Hank barked. "We're going after it."

"That's actually a good plan," Murphy commented, knowing that doing so would enable them to bring *The Thunder's* much more powerful, forward weapons to bear on the giant creature.

"Glad you approve," Corporal Hank scoffed at her.

****

The *Lady Freedom* was burning through what fuel she had left as Skipper pushed the yacht to her limits. Her engines roared and strained, hurling the boat over the water of the loch with as much speed as they could muster. Skipper stood on her bridge, keeping her course steady and hoping that the monster would be going after *The Thunder* and not his boat.

Weston and Marian were on the *Lady Freedom*'s deck, both armed, and praying that they wouldn't have to test the effectiveness of the weapons in their hands against the Loch Ness Monster. Marian clutched a .30-.06 hunting rifle in a white knuckled grip. Weston was armed with a .275 Rigby Highland Stalker rifle. It was made to shoot deer with but the rifle was the only other weapon aboard the boat that had any real range. Weston was also carrying a pump action shotgun, slung onto his back by its strap. If the monster got in close, they were likely dead but he dang well didn't plan on going out without a fight.

In the distance, explosions erupted in the loch, drawing Weston and Marian's attention to them.

"Looks like they hit the bastard," Weston commented.

"Hope they killed it," Marian muttered, even though she knew that the creature was likely humanity's only hope of surviving the virus that was reanimating the dead and turning them into dark, hungry monsters with a taste for human flesh.

"They didn't!" Weston yelped as he saw the huge shape of the monster beneath the water's surface break away from its pursuit of the torpedo boat and veer toward them. "It's coming our way!"

Weston left his position at the rear of the *Lady Freedom*, running closer to her bridge where hopefully Skipper could hear him better inside the yacht's bridge.

"Skipper!" Weston shouted. "That thing out there is coming at us! You better pick up the speed!"

"Can't!" Skipper yelled back at him. "We're already going full out. You're going to have to deal with it!"

Cursing Weston worked the bolt of his rifle to chamber a round, and then spat, "Well, that sucks."

"Weston!" Marian cried out, shrieking his name at the top of her lungs.

Already running back to her side, Weston saw why. The monster was closing on the *Lady Freedom* even faster than he had thought it would be able to. In another minute or so, the creature would be on top of them. He reached the edge of the boat's aft deck and dropped into a firing position there, on one knee, bracing his rifle and taking aim at the monster.

"Fragging shoot the thing!" Weston raged at Marian as he took his first shot. His rifle bucked in his hands as he pulled its trigger. Weston saw the round he fired splash into the water but couldn't tell if he had hit the approaching monster or not. Odds were he had but the thing hadn't even felt it. The creature was just so massive.

It was as if something snapped inside of Marian. Screaming in rage, she began to fire her .30-.06 over and over in rapid succession. Marian worked its bolt, ejecting spent shell casings and chambering fresh rounds, as quickly as she could. Each of the shots seemed to be perfect, striking the water directly where the giant monster swam towards them beneath its surface.

"Skipper!" Weston yelled as the monster picked up its speed even more, streaking towards the *Lady Freedom* like a bullet.

On the bridge, Skipper could see it coming too but there wasn't a blasted thing he could do about it. The *Lady Freedom's* engines were already past the red line and anything more would blow them for sure. He jerked the small yacht sharply to port, hoping to avoid the monster's fury but even as the *Lady Freedom* turned, the big man saw that it was too late. The yacht lurched as the giant monster struck it. Her hull cracked, wood splintering, metal bending and giving way. The monster tore straight through her mid-section, severing the yacht in two. Both ends jutted upwards in the water of the loch, already beginning to slowly sink as the monster, which had continued onward without slowing, swung around to come back towards them.

Weston was flung from the *Lady Freedom's* deck. He splashed into the ice-cold water of the loch. His rifle was gone. He'd lost it. The cold was so intense that it had taken his breath away. Weston struggled to stay afloat and conscious. Weston knew he was in shock. As he thrashed, Weston saw Marian nearby. He started to call out to her but then realized that the thin blonde woman was dead. Her body was floating, face down, with a jagged piece of the *Lady Freedom*'s deck protruding from the back. Marian's corpse bobbed up and down in the water. He knew Marian was going to reanimate soon. Weston desperately wanted to show her mercy and stop that from happening but Marian's body was out of reach, even if he could manage to get the knife sheathed on his belt free. Weston sunk for a moment, going under. Lunging back up, gasping for air, he saw the monster on its way back. It was even more frightening to see when you were staring directly into its face. Two massive, glowing, purple eyes seemed not to notice Weston at all as the monster continued to surge towards him. Using all the strength he had left, Weston swam frantically, trying to escape the monster but there was no escaping it. The monster rammed into him, breaking his bones, and ending his life, sending his mangled corpse spinning away from it.

The forward section of the *Lady Freedom* was sinking. It sat at an angle in the water, slipping ever so slowly downward in the icy depths. A good portion of it was still above the frigid surface for the time being though, including her bridge where Skipper clung to her steering console for dear life, keeping himself from sliding downward with his right hand. His left leg was bent unnaturally at his knee. The white of bone poked through the cloth of his pants there and his blood poured from the wound. Skipper's face was a twisted grimace of pain and determination. The big man had no intention of dying. He'd survived the zombie apocalypse after all and refused to let some fragging sea monster take him out.

Skipper managed to pull himself up enough to right his body and get into a safer position where he was no longer slipping. There was an emergency kit on the bridge and Skipper shifted his body so that was within his reach. Taking out the kit, the big man ignored its first aid contents knowing that he couldn't do much for his arm without help. Instead, Skipper dug out the flare gun from among the kit's contents. The damn, bloody monster that had killed the people under his protection and smashed apart the *Lady Freedom* was going to pay. He made it out of the bridge and onto the yacht's deck. The giant monster passed by the *Lady Freedom's* wreckage again at such speed its wake shoved the half of her Skipper was on through the water as the thing's massive form smashed the other half to pieces of broken wood and metal that spun like shrapnel through the air. He nearly lost his grip on the railing he was clutching but managed to hold on instead of sliding down the wet, splintered wood of the deck.

The monster wasn't done with what was left of the *Lady Freedom*. It had turned and was coming back again to finish the last of her, barreling through the water of the loch towards the section of the yacht he was on. Skipper took aim at the giant monster. The flare gun was the only weapon he had. He prayed the monster would raise its head above water with its mouth open like the shark in Jaws. Life wasn't a movie though and the monster was a blasted sight smarter than any Great White. His only hope of actually hitting the giant creature with the flare and hurting it was to take his shot the exact moment that the monster rammed into the section of the yacht he was on. The impact, he hoped at least, would force the monster's head up above the water. Skipper steadied his hand and steeled himself, waiting for that moment to come. There would be no escape for him regardless. He was dead no matter what happened. Between the cold of the water and his shattered leg, he'd never survive for help from *The Thunder* to reach him. They'd have to deal with the monster before they could even try. The only thing that mattered to him now was hurting the monster. Skipper knew his little flare gun couldn't kill it but he wanted to make sure that the creature knew he was spitting at it with his last breath.

To his surprise, the monster raised its head on its approach. He stared into the thing's glowing purple eyes as he took his shot, aiming for one of them. Something caught the flare in the air as it streaked towards the monster and knocked it aside as though it had been slapped aside by an invisible hand. Then the monster crashed into the section of the *Lady Freedom* he was on and the Skipper died.

****

Andrews had aimed *The Thunder* straight at the giant monster, chasing her at maximum speed but was forced to slow down and back off as the creature engaged the *Lady Freedom*. Everyone aboard *The Thunder* watched in horror as the monster destroyed her, first breaking the yacht in half with a single hit, and then coming around to smash apart what was left. Agent Murphy had held her fire with the torpedo boat's primary weapons, unwilling to risk the lives of anyone who might have survived aboard the *Lady Freedom*. The monster had just finished taking out what remained of the yacht and was coming back their way.

"You still feel anyone alive over there?" Murphy asked Cato.

Cato shook his head. "No," he answered sadly. "They're all dead now."

"There was nothing we could do," Andrews muttered, as if he was trying to convince himself of that fact.

"Agent Murphy, open fire on that fragging thing!" Corporal Hank barked.

"With pleasure," Murphy grinned. Her fingers danced over the controls of the weapons console. Beneath the surface of the loch, *The Thunder*'s forward launchers spat twin torpedoes at the inbound giant monster.

"Torpedoes away!" Murphy shouted.

"Contact in five. . .four. . . three. . ." Cato counted down from the sonar console.

The monster zigged and zagged about in the water attempting to out maneuver the torpedoes but they retained their lock on it. Suddenly, the monster came to an abrupt halt, the torpedoes continuing to close on it. The water between the monster and the torpedoes hardened into something akin to a shield. They struck it, detonating, sending shockwaves rippling across the loch.

"What the frag just happened?" Corporal Hank demanded.

"That thing out there stopped the torpedoes. That's what happened," Murphy frowned.

"How?" Corporal Hank rasped.

"Hydrokineiss? Telekinesis? Does it matter?" Murphy said. "Neither of the torpedoes made contact with it."

"Shut up and hit the bastard thing with another volley!" Corporal Hank spat.

Murphy grunted in anger but carried out his order.

A second pair of torpedoes roared out of *The Thunder*'s launchers, locked onto the giant creature, streaking through the water of the loch. The monster held its position, allowing the torpedoes to close on it. Again, the torpedoes were stopped short of making contact with the monster, exploding against the invisible barrier blocking their path.

"The torpedoes failed to make contact again," Agent Cato reported.

"Frag it!" Corporal Hank raged.

"Uh guys. . ." Andrews said. "You better take a look outside."

Agent Romona Romy, on the forward deck of *The Thunder,* watched as the monster shot towards the torpedo boat through the water, stopping just short of it. The monster rose up, breaking the surface of the loch. The fifty feet or so of its body above the water writhed about like a snake as dozens of tentacles unfurled from its sides. Burning, purple eyes looked down upon her as the monster towered over *The Thunder*.

Agent Engler came running from the boat's rear. The automatic shotgun he had looted from *The Thunder*'s stash of weapons after coming aboard boomed in a series of continuous thunderclaps. The monster barely flinched as the heavy slugs hammered into the mass of its central body. They were just too small to do much damage to something its size.

There were four tentacles which were much longer than all the others. They looked to function as if they were the monster's arms. One of them lashed out at Agent Engler. It slashed downward into him, pulping his body against the deck of the torpedo boat. Gore and Engler's entrails splattered out from beneath it. Romona wondered if Engler had tried to use his chronokinesis in order to escape his fate. . . if so, he had failed to do so in time or the monster had somehow blocked his power.

Agent Cato and the others emerged from *The Thunder*'s bridge, joining the fight, as Romona let loose on the monster with the .50 caliber machine gun she was manning. The rounds she fired sparked as they struck the telekinetic shield the creature hastily formed to protect itself. As a telekinetic herself, Romona could feel the strength of the barrier and knew that nothing aboard *The Thunder* in terms of conventional weapons was going to be able to pierce it.

Corporal Hank fired his rifle at the monster. Andrews followed his example. Their weapons were just as ineffective as Romona's. She had stopped firing with the .50, knowing that it was pointless. Agent Murphy just stood on the deck, helplessly, staring up at the giant creature which towered over them all.

It was Cato who was able to truly attack the monster, taking even Romona by surprise.

STOP! Cato's mental voice bellowed with such a level of raw strength that it knocked everyone else on the deck of *The Thunder* to their knees, clutching their heads. The monster recoiled from the young telepath, it too caught off guard by the sheer intensity of his power.

You have true power young one, Cato and all the others heard the monster's mental voice respond to his cry.

There's no need for any of this, Cato told the monster. *We're not here to fight you. We need your help.*

The monster gave a mental snort. *You think I don't know why you are here? I know the plans your doctor has for me very well. Cline wants my blood ... at any cost. And I shall not give it.*

Why? Cato pleaded. *You could save our entire race from extinction without it really costing you anything.*

So you *say little one,* the monster challenged Cato, *but have you not considered that this virus killing your kind might be of my creation?*

What? Why would you. . ? Cato gasped.

Your kind only kills and ruins, the monster bellowed, rearing up higher out of the water of the loch above the torpedo boat. *I have grown sick of watching you rape and destroy the world.*

There are so few of us left now, Cato argued. *Save us and give us a chance to start over. We can do better.*

No, the monster replied flatly and coldly.

Then you leave us no choice, Cato warned. *We will destroy you if we must.*

The monster gave a telepathic chuckle.

A psionically created portal shimmered into existence on the deck of the torpedo. It opened onto the sprawling streets of some distant city . . .and those streets were teeming with the dead. Rotting corpses, wailing in hunger, came pouring through the portal.

"Frag!" Andrews yelped as everyone but Cato and Romona whirled about to engage the dead.

"Take 'em out!" Corporal Hank yelled.

Murphy, who had been closest to the opening portal, was knocked from her feet and swarmed as the dead poured over her, clawing at her flesh, teeth ripping chunks of it away.

Cato's attention remained focused solely on the giant monster as its was on him. The two of them struggled in a battle of wills, each trying to force the other's mind into submission.

Romona could feel the mental shockwaves of their telepathic stabs traded between them. She had a plan of her own thanks to Cato keeping the monster distracted. The giant creature's telekinetic shield protecting its body was down, all its energies consumed in its battle with Cato and keeping open the portal through which the dead were boarding *The Thunder*. She reached out with her mind, touching the surface-to-surface missile launcher in the center of the torpedo boat and moved it around on its turret to target the monster. Concentrating, straining, Romona telekinetically fired the weapon. An anti-ship missile erupted from the launcher, hurtling into the monster's central mass. The missile struck the creature like a massive spear, sinking into its flesh, before exploding. The blast tore the upper part of the monster apart, sending chunks of flaming meat flying in every direction. The stump of the monster's body that was still above the surface of the loch toppled over, splashing into the water.

Cato collapsed from the sudden shock of being freed from the mental combat he had been engaged in. Romona rushed to his side, helping him to his feet.

"No time to rest yet, kid," she told him.

Corporal Hank and Andrews had been fighting a losing battle against the dead emerging from the portal the monster had created. The portal had closed when it died but there were already dozens of the dead aboard the torpedo boat that had pressed their way forward into melee range with the two soldiers. A dead man with half a face grabbed hold of Corporal Hank's rifle, shoving its barrel downwards. Bullets sparked against the boat's deck. Another of the dead moved past the one wrestling with the corporal, charging Andrews and tackling him. The two of them went down with Andrews beneath the rotting corpse. Its teeth tore open his throat in a spray of red.

Dr. Robert Cline screamed as a dead woman managed to lock the fingers of both her hands around his arm. Her teeth snapped in hunger as she tried to bite him and he struggled to fight her back. Romona hammered the dead woman with a blast of telekinetic force that caved in the woman's skull. The dead woman released her grip on Robert as she collapsed, now truly dead, onto the deck at his feet.

Cato was unconscious - his power wouldn't have affected the dead anyway as they had no minds for him to mess with but Romona could have still used him. And Dr. Cline was in shock, rendering him useless in the battle with the dead as well. That left only her and Corporal Hank to rid *The Thunder* of the dead that had come aboard her through the portal.

Corporal Hank wrested his rifle free from the rotting creature that was trying to take it from him. He swung the butt of the weapon up into the dead thing's chin, shattering it. The dead man staggered backwards as Corporal Hank laid into him again. Thrusting the butt of the rifle forward, Corporal Hank smashed in the dead man's forehead as bone crunched from the force of his blow. He didn't have time to be grateful for the small victory as several of the dead behind the one he had just taken out rushed him. Jagged fingernails clawed open his flesh as numerous cold, rotting hands clutched him, pulling him into the mass of the hungry dead. Teeth tore at his body, taking away chunks of his shoulders and cheeks. Corporal Hank died screaming as the dead ripped him apart.

Romona decided that she'd had enough of the foul creatures. With the Loch Ness Monster

dealt with, there was no reason to conserve her strength. She thrust both her hands outward in the direction of the dead. A wave of telekinetic force smashed into the dead like the shockwave of a detonating nuclear bomb. Their bones snapped inside of their decaying forms, brains pulped inside their skulls, and bodies flung from the deck of *The Thunder* as it hit them.

Dropping to her knees, Romona was spent. Sweat slicked her body and her head was pounding with pain. She saw Dr. Cline looking at her with an expression of awe.

"The monster's dead, doc," Romona told him. "Get whatever you need from it and let's get the hell out of here."

****

Two days later, Dr. Robert Cline found himself back inside the Temple. Surviving agents of the Order of the Eternal Life had retaken the base. Cato had gathered them, reaching out with his vast telepathic powers, summoning them to their aid.

Dr. Cline had been able to collect some of the Loch Ness Monster's blood with Romona's help. The powerful telekinetic had lifted its corpse up from the deep waters for him to take what he needed. His research was going well and promised to yield the results he had hoped for in a matter of days.

If all went well, soon, the dead would be dead once more . . . and the Earth would belong to what remained of the human race again.

The End

Eric S Brown is the author of numerous book series including the Bigfoot War series, the Psi-Mechs Inc. series, the Kaiju Apocalypse series (with Jason Cordova), the Crypto-Squad series (with Jason Brannon), the Homeworld series (With Tony Faville and Jason Cordova), the Jack Bunny Bam series, and the A Pack of Wolves series. Some of his stand alone books include War of the Worlds plus Blood Guts and Zombies, Casper Alamo (with Jason Brannon), Sasquatch Island, Day of the Sasquatch, Bigfoot, Crashed, World War of the Dead, Last Stand in a Dead Land, Sasquatch Lake, Kaiju Armageddon, Megalodon, Megalodon Apocalypse, Kraken, Alien Battalion, The Last Fleet, and From the Snow They Came to name only a few. His short fiction has been published hundreds of times in the small press in beyond including markets like the Onward Drake and Black Tide Rising anthologies from Baen Books, the Grantville Gazette, the SNAFU Military horror anthology series, and Walmart World magazine. He has done the novelizations for such films as Boggy Creek: The Legend is True (Studio 3 Entertainment) and The Bloody Rage of Bigfoot (Great Lake films). The first book of his Bigfoot War series was adapted into a feature film by Origin Releasing in 2014. Werewolf Massacre at Hell's Gate was the second of his books to be adapted into film in 2015. Major Japanese publisher, Takeshobo, bought the reprint rights to his Kaiju Apocalypse series (with Jason Cordova) and the mass market, Japanese language version was released in late 2017. Ring of Fire Press has released a collected edition of his Monster Society stories (set in the New York Times Best-selling world of Eric Flint's 1632). In addition to his fiction, Eric also writes an award-winning comic book news column entitled "Comics in a Flash" as well a pop culture column for Altered Reality Magazine. Eric lives in North Carolina with his wife and two children where he continues to write tales of the hungry dead, blazing guns, and the things that lurk in the woods.

CHECK OUT OTHER GREAT DEEP SEA THRILLERS

THE BREACH
by Edward J. McFadden III

A Category 4 hurricane punched a quarter mile hole in Fire Island, exposing the Great South Bay to the ferocity of the Atlantic Ocean, and the current pulled something terrible through the new breach. A monstrosity of the past mixed with the present has been disturbed and it's found its way into the sheltered waters of Long Island's southern sea.

Nate Tanner lives in Stones Throw, Long Island. A disgraced SCPD detective lieutenant put out to pasture in the marine division because of his Navy background and experience with aquatic crime scenes, Tanner is assigned to hunt the creeper in the bay. But he and his team soon discover they're the ones being hunted.

INFESTATION
by William Meikle

It was supposed to be a simple mission. A suspected Russian spy boat is in trouble in Canadian waters. Investigate and report are the orders.

But when Captain John Banks and his squad arrive, it is to find an empty vessel, and a scene of bloody mayhem.

Soon they are in a fight for their lives, for there are things in the icy seas off Baffin Island, scuttling, hungry things with a taste for human flesh.

They are swarming. And they are growing.

"Scotland's best Horror writer" - Ginger Nuts of Horror

"The premier storyteller of our time." - Famous Monsters of Filmland

CHECK OUT OTHER GREAT DEEP SEA THRILLERS

SHARK: INFESTED WATERS
by P.K. Hawkins

For Simon, the trip was supposed to be a once in a lifetime gift: a journey to the Amazon River Basin, the land that he had dreamed about visiting since he was a child. His enthusiasm for the trip may be tempered by the poor conditions of the boat and their captain leading the tour, but most of the tourists think they can look the other way on it. Except things go wrong quickly. After a horrific accident, Simon and the other tourists find themselves trapped on a tiny island in the middle of the river. It's the rainy season, and the river is rising. The island is surrounded by hungry bull sharks that won't let them swim away. And worst of all, the sharks might not be the only blood-thirsty killers among them. It was supposed to be the trip of a lifetime. Instead, they'll be lucky if they make it out with their lives at all.

DARK WATERS
by Lucas Pederson

Jörmungandr is an ancient Norse sea monster. Thought to be purely a myth until a battleship is torn a part by one.

With his brother on that ship, former Navy Seal and deep-sea diver, Miles Raine, sets out on a personal vendetta against the creature and hopefully save his brother. Bringing with him his old Seal team, the Dagger Points, they embark on a mission that might very well be their last.

But what happens when the hunters become the hunted and the dark waters reveal more than a monster?

CHECK OUT OTHER GREAT DEEP SEA THRILLERS

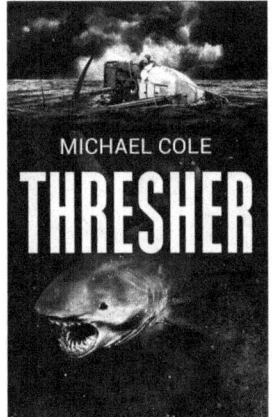

THRESHER
by **Michael Cole**

In the aftermath of a hurricane, a series of strange events plague the coastal waters off Florida. People go into the water and never return. Corpses of killer whales drift ashore, ravaged from enormous bite marks. A fishing trawler is found adrift, with a mysterious gash in its hull.

Transferred to the coastal town of Merit, police officer Leonard Riker uncovers the horrible reality of an enormous Thresher shark lurking off the coast. Forty feet in length, it has taken a territorial claim to the waters near the town harbor. Armed with three-inch teeth, a scythe-like caudal fin, and unmatched aggression, the beast seeks to kill anything sharing the waters.

THE GUILLOTINE
by **Lucas Pederson**

1,000 feet under the surface, Prehistoric Anthropologist, Ash Barrington, and his team are in the midst of a great archeological dig at the bottom of Lake Superior where they find a treasure trove of bones. Bones of dinosaurs that aren't supposed to be in this particular region. In their underwater facility, Infinity Moon, Ash and his team soon discover a series of underground tunnels. Upon exploring, they accidentally open an ice pocket, thawing the prehistoric creature trapped inside. Soon they are being attacked, the facility falling apart around them, by what Ash knows is a dunkleosteus and all those bones were from its prey. Now...Ash and his team are the prey and the creature will stop at nothing to get to them.

www.ingramcontent.com/pod-product-compliance
Lightning Source LLC
Chambersburg PA
CBHW061249170626
46809CB00007B/2918